PROTECTOR

LOLA
TAYLOR

If there's one thing Nik Johnson can't stand, it's the thought of finding his mate. Which, apparently, he'll have to do soon, since his mating Fever has finally arrived. With his thoughts still hung up on his former lover, he's given up the hope of ever finding a love that perfect again. Until he meets Alara....

Alara Crescent has had anything but a charmed life, despite her family's status as high family within the werewolf world. Ridiculed constantly for her weight by her cruel mother and father, she's beginning to wonder if she'll ever be accepted for who she truly is. Then one fateful encounter delivers her right into the arms of the man she's destined to have.

When someone starts assassinating the royal family, Nik takes it upon himself to protect the woman he's marked—a woman who would as soon bite him as love him. Despite their prejudices, can the two of them find true love before the Blood Moon rises?

Cover designed by Kitten of Deranged Doctor Design
Interior design and formatting by Champagne Formats
Editing by Jen of Mistress Editing
Indigo Dreamer Press logo designed by Indi99o of 99designs
Author photograph by Sara Rogers Photography

www.lolataylorbooks.com
www.indigodreamerpress.com

INDIGO
DREAMER PRESS

ISBN-10: 0-9835131-6-3
ISBN-13: 978-0-9835131-6-2

For more information, please visit
www.lolataylorbooks.com

CHAPTER ONE

F ALL NEEDED TO SLOW THE HELL DOWN. NIK JOHNSON couldn't believe it had already been three weeks since he, his brother, and the young werewolf Jason had fought Onyx for Danica's life. Things had been eerily peaceful since.

And if life had taught Nik anything, it was that peace never lasted for long.

He gripped the steering wheel of the Honda Odyssey, his jaw clenching. They'd had no more leads on Mistress Black since the incident. Not even the DPI was able to uncover anything. Nik suspected the witch mafia had gone dark to cover their tracks. Smart move. He would've done the same in their shoes.

It still wouldn't stop him ripping their throats out with his jaws when the time came.

You thinking about the mafia again? came Gage's voice in his head.

Nik glanced in the rearview mirror, catching his younger brother's worried eyes. *Reading minds now, Your Highness?*

Gage's jaw ticked as it always did at the mention of his formal title. Nik liked to dig it in just for shits and giggles. *Something will turn up. That's one of the reasons we're going to this summit.*

We're going because we have no other choice. It's not like we can ignore a summons from the High King, Nik said, scowling. *And I'm only going to bail your ass out of trouble.*

Who says I'm looking for trouble?

We're Johnson brothers. Since when does trouble not *come find us?*

Gage grinned. *Point made.*

What are you two talking about? came Danica's voice. The lovely blonde looked more luminous than ever now that she was nearing her first Change. Nik could tell Gage was anxious; he hadn't taken his hand off her thigh since they got in the car and started driving over an hour ago. The champagne-colored ball gown she wore flared at the hips slightly, the taffeta skirt inlaid with silver beading and glittering green vines that matched the hue of her startling eyes. Her swirling, dark-blue Mark shimmered down her arms and along her chest and upper back. She was radiant. Nik couldn't be more proud of her, of the queen she'd become.

Nothing, lil sis, Nik assured her. *Just telling my baby brother how dazzling the two of you look together.* Gage's tux and dark hair complemented Danica's lighter look, like light and darkness.

Danica giggled. Nik enjoyed making her smile. She'd been through so much. *I'm sure, tiger.*

Jason put down his Nintendo 3DS and turned around in his seat beside Nik. "Man, am I missing out on a wolf conversation again?" In the tux, he looked a lot younger than he was, like he was going to prom and not a summit for all the packmasters.

"Don't worry," Gage said, winking at him. "You didn't miss out on anything too exciting. Just more of Nik's brooding."

"I am *not* brooding," Nik said. "I'm just thinking about how much I'm going to dread seeing this lot of egotistical, pompous assholes."

Danica pouted. "We're not egotistical."

"Don't worry, love," Nik said. "You're the only royals I can stand."

"Hey, look on the bright side," Gage said, slapping him on the shoulder. "Maybe you'll find your mate. I know your Fever hasn't come yet, but you never can tell."

Nik swallowed hard, pasting on a devil-may-care smile. "I think our boy Jason here has a better chance at finding a mate than I do. How's that Fever treating you? Had any more wet dreams?"

Jason's Fever had come full-force at the beginning of the month. His face heated and he flipped them the bird, which only made Nik and Gage snicker. Jason's reaction only reminded Nik of how young and inexperienced with women the pup was, despite his ranking within the pack. After defeating Onyx, Gage had officially promoted Nik as his Beta and Jason as his Delta. Jason may not be the strongest were in the pack, but he was far more courageous and loyal than those other sons of bitches they called packmates.

Gage sat back, talking quietly with his mate. He tenderly brushed a blond curl from her face, and she giggled, kissing him.

Nik smiled sadly and focused on the open road, on the late afternoon sunshine warming his face, on anything but finding his mate. Truth was, his Fever had come at the start of the month too—he just hadn't told Gage. His chest tightened. Gage and he shared everything, but this was the one thing he wouldn't understand. He didn't know what it was like to have burned with love for someone so deeply it reached your core, only to have them torn away from you because it wasn't what was written in the werewolf laws. He and Verika, no matter how perfect, were never meant to be.

And that knowledge killed a little bit more of him every day whenever he thought of her smile or her red hair. Nik didn't care what the damn Fever said—whomever he marked would never be Verika. Nik knew, if he were being honest with himself, that was another reason he hadn't told Gage about getting his Fever. He didn't want Gage pressuring him into finding a mate, which he knew he would be inclined to do now that he'd found his. Nik had been dreading this moment ever since he and Verika broke up. He was tempted to not even try and just let the Blood Moon come and go, cursing him with the inability to ever fall in love again. That was a lovely little spin the bitch of a witch who created the Curse of the Moon

4

decided to throw in.

"Whoa," Danica said, sitting up and pointing. "Is that it? The High King's castle?"

"Castle Crescent," Gage said, eyeing the fifteenth-century replica, complete with turrets and torches. "He had it brought over from Scotland, stone by stone, and rebuilt here."

"It's beautiful," Danica said, then she smiled. "You guys have a thing for naming places after the moon, don't you?"

Gage shrugged. "The night is in our blood, though we can shift at any time."

Nik drummed his fingers along the steering wheel. He was almost grateful to see the sprawling castle. A party meant booze, and he was in dire need of a drink right about now.

He pulled into the drive, past rows of pruned rosebushes, and drove to the front of the castle, where a veritable drawbridge sat. Traffic moved along steadily as more werewolves arrived for the gathering, and Nik parked up front. Valets opened their doors, and Nik handed one the keys.

"Wow," Danica said, her arm looped through her mate's as they walked across the drawbridge. "This is incredible." She peered over the side into the stream flowing past.

"Don't worry," Nik said with a wink. "No alligators. Only koi."

Butlers decked out in tuxedos and wearing the golden crescent-shaped pin of the House of Crescent, the ruling werewolf family, handed out champagne flutes at the door as guests entered the foyer.

It had been a long time since Nik had been to Castle Crescent. Despite his reservations about the people who lived here, he had to admit the place was pretty cool. It was just like stepping back in time and entering a medieval castle. All the architecture had been restored. Frescoes of the heavens, with skies swirling with angels at war, dominated the ceilings. Grand iron chandeliers set with electric candles hung from the ceiling, though torches and candelabra lit with real fire dotted the walls. Tapestries that cost more money than Crescent Manor's mortgage hung along the walls, and indigo banners bearing the House Crescent coat of arms—a crescent moon, a sword, and a rose—hung from the wooden rafters. The air smelled of roses, enormous vases of which lined the room. People dressed in gowns of silk and tuxedos stood about the room, making polite conversation. From the grand ballroom beyond, Nik could see dancers twirling away to the lilting waltz provided by the live orchestra.

The high family sure didn't spare any expense at these things. It seemed like such a waste of money, all the packmasters gathered here so they could kiss ass with the High King and learn things they already knew. The werewolf community didn't exactly have a monthly werewolf e-zine or anything, but word got around about important things.

Like Gage's mate almost being murdered in cold blood.

Nik felt Gage tense as an elegant man with jet-black hair streaked with gray approached. The silver flower of the Nightshade Pack was pinned to his lapel. Gage and Nik stepped in front of Danica, Jason standing guard next to her. The three of them moved at once, a well-trained unit, finely attuned to one another's emotions and movements.

The man paused, blinked, then chuckled. "Come now, Gage. Surely you aren't going to sic your watchdogs on me?"

Nik growled and Jason coughed, "Bastard."

"That depends on the reason you're approaching me, Norman," Gage said with icy formality. "Come to explain to me why one of your pack tried to kill my mate last month?"

"Did you not receive my letter?" Norman said, feigning surprise. "Must have gotten lost in the mail."

"There's this thing we use in the twenty-first century called email. Or the telephone," Nik added. "Hell, even a text would've been better than nothing. You do know how to text, right, Grandpa?"

Norman sneered at him. "Do not address me so informally, Beta. I am still an Alpha, regardless of your distaste for me." He turned his granite eyes back on Gage. "I do not know anything about Onyx's activities with the witches. I do not police my pack's personal affairs."

"Maybe you should," Gage growled. "Then we might have avoided all this. And I'm still waiting on you to say you're sorry, that you're glad my mate's alive." Gage took a step forward so only a few inches stood between their eyes. "You are glad she's alive, aren't you?"

"Are you insinuating I had something to do with this?"

"You tell me."

"Enough!"

Everyone turned toward the grand staircase, seeing a tall man with a graying beard staring down at them. He wore what appeared to be a military uniform, complete with gold brocade and a sword at his side. A crimson sash was secured across his chest, seeming brighter against the indigo of his jacket and white pants.

A trumpet sounded and someone announced, "Your king! His Highness Victor Crescent!"

The whole room bowed or curtsied. Danica glanced around, looking nervous. Nik whispered in her ear, "You're doing great. Just breathe."

She smiled back. *Thanks*, she said through their pack-link.

"Please, carry on," Victor said, and the orchestra picked up its tune again. The room was once more filled with multiple conversations, though several curious eyes lingered on Gage and Nik, anticipating a fight, no doubt.

Nik eyed Norman with loathing, hating to disappoint. He wondered how long it would take the guards to wrestle him to the floor if he were to get in one good punch….

Don't even think about it, Gage warned.

What? Little innocent me? I'm docile as a kitten.

Gage snorted.

As Victor approached, their party turned and bowed. "Your Majesty," Norman said, "what an extravagant—"

"Save it, Black," Victor snapped with a careless flick of his wrist. "Your flattery will not work on me."

Norman's thin lips pinched shut as heat rose to his cheeks. Nik resisted the urge to snicker.

Victor's sharp gaze roved over them, landing on Danica. They narrowed slightly. "So this is the queen who's caused such a stir among our community."

Danica swallowed hard, going rigid as the High King motioned her forward. Nik gave her an encouraging nudge, and she took a few hesitant steps. She began to curtsy, keeping her eyes on the floor, but Victor stopped her.

"No need for formalities, my dear," he said, not without kindness. "I just wanted a better look at you. It's unusual for a human to be marked by an Alpha."

"So I'm told," she said, a little breathier, a nervous habit of hers, Nik noted.

Victor smiled. "You're well worth the trouble, I'm sure. Though I'm sorry to hear we lost so many wolves in that senseless battle."

"As am I, Your Majesty," Gage said quietly.

"And I," Norman added quickly.

Nik rolled his eyes. Of course he was sorry now. He was just putting on a show for the king, that's all.

"Good," Victor said. "You can show how sorry you are by paying the retribution tax to the Moonstruck Pack. Since I've been in touch with the DPI's Chief of Police, there is no need to go to trial because we know for a fact Onyx was guilty. The standard penalty for an attack on another pack's members is one hundred thousand dollars."

"*What*?" Norman roared. "That's outrageous! She's just a human!"

The guards rested their hands on the guns at their holsters as Victor drew himself to his full height. "But not anymore," he said in a low tone. "You either obey my laws or lose your position as Alpha within your pack. Which is it?"

Norman's face turned red with fury, and his fists shook at his sides. "Very well," he said tightly, downing the last of his champagne. "I shall have our secretary forward the money over." With that, he bowed to the king, muttering, "Your Majesty," then spun on his heel and stormed out the doors.

Victor slapped a hand on Gage's shoulder. "Don't worry about the Nightshade Pack. I've been aware of Norman's shady dealings in the Underworld for years, but we never seem to have enough evidence to officially charge him with anything. I will say, the man is clever when it comes to getting others to do his dirty work for him. You have any trouble out of him, come straight to me, understand?"

"Yes, Your Highness," Gage said, nodding. "Thank you."

Victor nodded curtly, then turned on a smile for his other guests as he walked away, surrounded by his guards.

Danica's shoulders slumped with relief. "Oh, my gosh, he's so intimidating! I felt like Cinderella standing before the king."

"Good thing it's the prince who matters in that tale," Gage said, pulling her to his side and kissing her forehead.

"Get a room!" Nik said dramatically when a sultry voice stopped him cold.

"You son of a bitch."

He turned just in time to see a hand flying toward

his face. With lightning-quick reflexes, he grabbed the woman's thin wrist before she could slap him. She was well-muscled, typical of she-wolves, with light brown hair that shone with gold highlights. Her blue eyes stared back at him with fury. "Shawna," Nik said with an inward grimace.

"Oh, so you do remember me." She jerked her hand free of his grasp and crossed her arms, making her small breasts bunch against the fabric of her violet gown. "Where the hell do you get off sleeping with me, then leaving before the sun's even risen?"

A gentleman whistled low nearby, and Nik shot him a warning glare. He hastily turned around and walked his date back in the opposite direction.

Nik forced patience into his voice. "Shawna, you knew what you were getting into when you came home with me from Howl that night. You know I'm not a cuddling, breakfast-in-bed kind of guy."

"No, you're apparently a bag 'em and leave 'em kind of guy." She spit in his face. "I sure hope whoever your mate is knows what the hell she's getting herself into with you—a lifetime of hurt."

Nik felt that cut to the bone, and he had to fight not to show it. He'd often wondered since Verika left if maybe he just wasn't good enough—maybe not for anyone. He wasn't enough. It was ludicrous because of the laws of the Fever and marking a mate, but the little voice of doubt liked to whittle away at his already tarnished self-esteem.

Shawna turned and stalked off in the other direction.

Gage sighed, shaking his head. "Shawna, Nik? Really?"

Nik pushed aside his inner turmoil and pasted on a charming smile, just like he always did. "What? She was drunk. I was drunk. We were horny. It seemed like a win-win situation."

"She's an Alpha, one of the few female Alphas in our region."

"I know. And let me tell you, she's not that dominant in bed."

"Nik," Danica chastised.

"All right, all right, I'll drop it." Nik took a sip of his champagne, looking around. "Where's the kid?"

"I dunno," Gage said, glancing around as well. "He said something about slipping off to find the bathroom, and I haven't seen him since."

"Slacking on the job already," Nik said with a wink.

Gage cast him a look that said, "You're impossible," then his gaze turned troubled.

Nik didn't have to ask to know what he was thinking about. "Yeah, so shall we mingle and shit and find some leads on our witch mafia friends?"

"I'm not sure how much help the other leaders will be," Gage said doubtfully. "Malachite burned a lot of bridges while he was Alpha."

"But you're not Malachite," Nik said, slapping a hand on his brother's shoulder. "And bridges can be rebuilt."

Gage smiled gratefully at him, straightening and looking more like the King of Wolves Nik knew him to be. "Right. Got to start somewhere."

Danica rested her hand on his arm and smiled up at her mate. "I'll go with you. I'm not afraid of some men, not in this dress."

Nik laughed. "There's my girl."

Gage glanced at his watch. "What do you say we circle the room, then meet back here in half an hour?"

"Sounds good. I'll start with the drink bar."

"Nik...."

"I know, I know. I won't get drunk and embarrass you. I'll be on my best behavior." He grinned and Gage shook his head.

"Why doesn't that make me feel any better?" he muttered.

Danica tugged at his arm. "Come on. Let's mingle."

Gage smiled at her adoringly and gave Nik one last nod as he led his mate away to a group of older pack leaders standing nearby.

Wise move, Nik thought as the group greeted Gage and Danica with smiles as he introduced the newest addition to his pack. The older werewolves were more secure in their power, having ruled for a few decades. They weren't intimidated by newcomers like some of the younger packmasters were, who could still be easily dislodged from power.

Nik was grateful at times like these that he wasn't an Alpha, nor did he ever want to be. He'd been leading for so long, taking care of Gage while they were growing up and all, that he'd lost an appetite for it. Let someone else lead for a change. He was content with sitting back and watching.

Glancing at his now-empty champagne flute, he made his way toward the refreshment bar, tuning his ears to any gossip that might give them a lead on the witch mafia.

And tuning his inner wolf away from searching for the mate he didn't want.

CHAPTER TWO

THE DAMN DRESS WOULDN'T FIT.

Alara stared at her reflection hopefully in the mirror as she tried in vain to zip the dress up. It had fit fine at a size sixteen, but of course soon as her mother had seen the size on the tag, she'd had the dress altered to fit a size smaller. And even that was too large for her appearance-driven mother, High Queen of all werewolves.

Tears pricked Alara's eyes as her frustration boiled over. On the verge of tearing the dress off, she heard the door open, and her mother, dripping in diamonds and silver gauze, swept into the room. One would never guess she had been one of the fiercest werewolves in their race's history.

Alara nearly gagged on the sharp perfume that clouded the air as her mother came up behind her and frowned. "You're late. Why aren't you dressed yet?"

"I told you—I had to study for an exam. And I'm not

dressed because the dress doesn't fit," Alara said without irritation.

Her mother rolled her eyes. "What exam? I thought you dropped that ridiculous online course."

"No, I told you since you wouldn't allow me to go to a college campus, I had to find a program to accept me online. I'm getting my general ed. courses over with."

"Why? What's the point? It's not like you're actually leaving us. You have an obligation—"

"To this pack," Alara finished tiredly. "I know, Mother. You've told me so every time I bring up wanting to be a veterinarian."

Her mother snorted. "Like a common human. Stop fussing with that zipper before you rip your dress."

Oh, what a travesty that would be, thought Alara dryly.

Steeling her jaw, she dropped her arms and tried to keep her disappointment at bay as her mother wrestled with the zipper. "Guests started arriving over a half hour ago. Honestly, Alara, when are you going to accept your place in this pack?"

When hell freezes over. "Sorry, Mother. I hate to disappoint you."

"Then why do you keep doing it?"

Alara blinked, but that was all the reaction she showed. *Feel numb. Numb takes the pain away.* "I don't know. I have this dream I can't get out of my head, I guess." She hated how childlike she sounded. She hated even more how much she wanted her mother's approval, even after knowing there was no way she'd get it.

"Dreams are for people without responsibility. And

you are the crown princess of the most ancient pack on this earth. Your duties lie with this pack before yourself."

"I know," Alara said, her chest tightening with the sensation her dreams were crumbling around her again.

"Ugh," her mother said with disgust as she worked the zipper up another inch. "What have you been eating for breakfast?"

"A nonfat fruit parfait, Mother."

"What about dinner last night? Lunch?"

"Salad, Mother."

"Sssh, don't say anything. Suck in your gut, if you can manage that."

Be numb.

Alara inhaled as much as she could, bunching her generous breasts as her mother forced the zipper up. "You've been working out?" her mother went on.

Alara paused, unsure whether she should speak when her mother told her not to.

"Well?" her mother snapped. "Did you not hear me?"

"Yes," Alara said in a monotone voice. "Every day for two hours, just like Izzy."

"'Isabelle,'" her mother corrected. "'Izzy' is not the name of a princess. 'Isabelle' sounds much more regal. There!"

Alara gasped as the zipper reached its summit, thus compromising her ability to breathe. Her wolf ears could hear the fabric stretch every time she inhaled. Too much and she'd rip a seam.

Her mother continued examining her, grabbing her arm and holding it up. "And you haven't lost any weight?

Your biceps are jiggling. I'll have to speak to your trainer. Perhaps I should call Dr. Rolf again, get you on a different weight loss medication."

Alara sighed carefully. "You ever considered maybe I'm built this way for a reason? Maybe I'm not supposed to be rail-thin."

Her mother leveled her with an even glare. "If you're going to be a royal were—one of the high family, at that—there is a certain physical standard of beauty we have to uphold. And 'fat' is not it."

Alara looked down at her body, at the skin bunched around her arms, hanging over the corset's rim. She was hardly fat. Sure, she wore a few sizes higher than most she-wolves because she had a round bottom, big, full breasts, and wide hips—and okay, maybe she sported a few more curves around the midsection, too—but come on!

Her mother's ruby lips pursed. "If I'd known your arms looked like this, I never would have gone with a sleeveless dress." She sighed dramatically as if this was all very taxing to her. "No time to change. We'll just have to improvise." She went over to the massive dresser and produced a pair of above-the-elbow black lace gloves that complemented the black lace trimming in Alara's teal, puffy ball gown. "Here. Put these on. They'll draw the eye away from your fat."

Alara felt her cheeks heat as she obediently pulled on the gloves. They were feminine; the dress, despite its size restrictions, made her feel pretty. She smiled at herself in the mirror, her back straightening a bit. But her mother didn't see her as pretty. She saw her as a failure, a glaring neon sign of how different she was from other werewolves.

Sharp pain lit up her cheeks as her mother pinched her face. "Ow!" Alara said. "What was that for?"

"You're too pale," she said dismissively. "You need to have some color in you, look like you're an outdoors kind of woman to attract a suitable mate. Oh, to think! Twenty-two and unmated! And a *high were!*"

Alara gritted her teeth. You'd think they were in the 1800s and she was considered an old maid. It wasn't that she didn't want to find a mate. She just wanted it to be for the right reasons. Not that she'd have a choice in the matter. "I haven't marked anyone yet, and no one has marked me," Alara said simply.

Her mother chose to completely ignore this logic. "Well, it's hard to mark someone when you haven't had your Fever yet!"

"You're talking about it like it's my period."

"Don't say the 'p' word. Just because you've blossomed doesn't mean you're a full-fledged she-wolf yet."

"Mother," Alara groaned, "stop talking about people like they're plants. People don't 'blossom.' Besides, Isabelle hasn't had her Fever either."

"She's younger than you," her mother said, quick to defend the perfect younger sister.

"By a whole year," Alara drawled. "Two grown daughters, unmated." She covered her mouth, feigning shock. "People will start talking if you don't bend the universe to your will soon."

Her mother's even glare made her shut up.

Down girl.

"Enough stalling," her mother said, clapping her hands. "We have important guests waiting."

Alara almost said, "Let them wait," but instead, she gathered her skirts, straightened her back, and put her "princess face" on.

Smile. Make mind-numbingly polite conversation. Survive the drudgery of it all. She almost wished she'd hurry up and get her Fever. At least then she might feel something for once.

Soon as she stepped into the hall, her resolve slipped a bit. A cluster of slender-bodied women in brightly-colored lace and silk approached, all congregated around the tall blonde in the middle. *Tiffany*, Alara thought with a growl.

They all stopped and curtsied low for the queen, casting frosty, fake smiles at Alara. "Your Highness," Tiffany drawled with a wink to her friends, "that color looks great on you."

Alara's anger flared. She knew Tiffany didn't like the color one bit—she was being snide. She'd been a viper since they played in the sandbox together. "Thanks, Tiffany," she said with the same mock enthusiasm. "I wish I could say the same for that Pepto-Bismol pink nightmare of yours."

The girls all gasped at once while her mother snapped, "Alara!"

Alara gave them a frosty nod and swept past them. When her mother called after her, she kept walking, in no mood for a lecture. Her mother should have defended her, not thrown her to the wolves, literally. She grew angrier with every step, the sight of those lean, toned girls a reminder of the world she didn't fit into.

"Alara! Wait up!"

Alara quickly composed herself and turned to see Isabelle floating toward her. Izzy always reminded her of Cinderella, the perfect fairy tale princess—who could snap your bones with a flick of her wrist.

Izzy's delicate pink lips pouted as she gazed at her sister with concerned blue eyes. "I'm sorry about them," she said in that sweet voice of hers. "They're usually really nice girls. I don't know why they get that way sometimes."

"I can tell you—because they're bitches."

"Alara…."

Alara sighed. "I know, I know. I'm sorry. I know they're your friends, but…." She took Izzy's hands. "Izzy, you're so sweet. I don't want anyone to take advantage of you."

"I won't let anyone take advantage of me," she said cheerily.

Alara just smiled back. Her poor, naive sister wouldn't have a clue if someone was taking advantage of her. She was entirely too trusting for this corrupt world of back-stabbing politics and power plays. The two girls had grown up thick as thieves, remaining close well into adulthood. Her mother had started prying them apart as she prepared them for their "separate roles." Alara would become High Queen someday, and Izzy would be married off to another royal were, no doubt. Members of the high family usually marked other royal werewolves, so both would marry well—if they could find their mates.

"You do look really pretty," Izzy said with a small smile.

Alara dropped her hands, looking away.

Izzy wasn't fooled. "You had another run-in with Mother, didn't you?"

Alara pressed her lips together. "It's nothing."

Izzy hugged her. People walked by, staring, but neither girl cared. "Don't pay her any attention," Izzy whispered. "You're perfect the way you are."

Alara hugged her sister back tightly, close to tears. She hadn't realized how much she'd yearned to hear that, to hear someone didn't find her repulsive. "Thank you."

They separated and Izzy grabbed her hand. "Come on. Let's get you some champagne."

Am I ever going to need it, Alara thought as her eager sister dragged her downstairs into the foyer.

The party was well underway with guests milling about in their finery. Alara thought it was all a bit ridiculous, a pissing contest among the royal werewolves, but this society of jewels and glitter was what she grew up in. They were stopped by a few patrons, at which Alara had to pretend to be happy to see their backstabbing asses. They all adored Izzy. She was usually the center of attention, no matter where they went. Beautiful and kind, she was the perfect lady. Alara wanted to hate her, but she couldn't. Izzy was too damn nice.

When it became awkwardly clear Alara wasn't going to be a part of the conversation, she quietly excused herself and made a beeline for the wine table. If she was expected to smile and pretend to be happy, then dammit she was getting buzzed.

She scooped up a glass and took a long sip when her

wolf senses tingled, and she looked up anxiously.

Gerard?

Her eyes landed on the source of the strange sensation, finding a tall, handsome man leaning against the opposite wall. And he was staring right at her. She let her gaze rove over him, inch by gorgeous inch. He was cleaned up, but she could tell by the scar running across his brow and the holes in his ears where multiple studs could be placed he had a wild side.

And something about that made her flush with heat.

She blinked. Usually, she wasn't the type to get all hot and bothered over a guy, but this one made her want to pant.

Dismissing her carnal urges to a fleeting fancy, she downed the rest of her wine. Then she retrieved another glass before disappearing into the crowd, the feel of the stranger's eyes hot on her back.

CHAPTER THREE

I T WAS LIKE A RADAR HIT HIM, WITH A TRACKER HONED in on the brunette across the room. Without shame, Nik let his sharp eyes rove over her body, the hem of the shiny teal silk suggesting plump curves. It was sexy. She looked healthy, like she actually had an appetite, unlike a lot of the human coat hangers strutting around like they owned the place.

He started to look away, to dismiss the woman as a fleeting fancy, when the thought of letting her out of his sight terrified him.

Go after her.

It was barely a thought, more like a whisper of his subconscious mind, but he followed her through the room. His inner wolf grew restless as he watched his prey, growling as another male came up to her and asked her to dance. He wasn't snooping, Nik told himself. He was merely curious, concerned for her well-being, even.

Since when the hell are you so chivalrous? came the taunting voice inside.

He quickly ignored it and continued watching the woman, smiling as she promptly rejected the man. He was pushy, a typical were. Nik listened, attentive but keeping his distance. That is, until the man put his hands on the woman.

Nik swiftly stepped forward. "She can't take the next dance with you because she's already promised it to me," he said smoothly, standing beside her and putting a hand on the small of her back.

The woman blinked up at him, looking surprised, but she didn't argue. "Yes," she finally said, "I'm sorry, Drake. Perhaps another time."

Nik gave a vicious smile to Drake as the other wolf sized him up.

Any time, any day, hot shot.

At last, Drake growled and turned, muttering something about "country wolves." The insult rolled off Nik like it always did. He was accustomed to it by now after dealing with royals for so long, the stuck-up lot.

Nik smiled down at his new companion, offering his arm. "Shall we?"

She stared at him. Her cherry lips had the perfect pout effect. He wanted to nibble on that succulent bottom lip…. "Shall we what?" she asked.

"Dance?" He gestured to the ballroom with his head. "You did just agree to it."

"I—I did not!"

"You did. Or do I need to go get Drake as a witness?"

She scowled at him. "I don't dance."

"You do now. Come on. One dance, that's all I ask." When she still made no answer, he added in a low, sing-song voice, "It'll be fun."

She swallowed hard, her pupils dilating slightly. "Fine. One dance. But if you so much as put your hands where they don't belong, I'll bite you."

"Oh, please do," he purred, and she dug her nails into his arm. He chuckled. He liked this one. She had the same "take no shit" attitude as the other she-wolves, but there was something more vulnerable about her. She looked like a fish out of water, so to speak. He could relate. He hated this whole ordeal as much as anyone.

The first strains of a new waltz floated through the air as they entered the ballroom and took their place among the dancers. "Come on," Nik said with a low laugh, pulling her close to him. "I wore cologne today and everything."

"Where are all your piercings?" she said with derision, eyeing his ears as they began to turn to the beat.

"In my jewelry box with all my other trinkets," he said, perfectly poker-faced.

She blinked, looking startled.

He chuckled, and she bit on her lip to hide her smile. "You're toying with me."

"Only because I like to see you smile."

She looked at him sharply. "What's the catch?"

"Catch?" he asked, taken off-guard.

"You know what I mean. What's in it for you, getting on my good side?"

"Well, if I'm lucky, the privilege of another dance," he

replied smoothly. He could dish out a lot of romantic bull-shit—anything to get a woman into his bed for a night of mindless sex—but thing was—he meant it. This time, he wasn't playing for a booty call.

A blush colored her pale cheeks, making him warmer. *Lovely.*

"What's your name?" he asked, pulling her closer so their chests were touching. This close, he could feel the press of her round, full breasts against him. Desire stirred deep in his gut, pushing blood south of his navel.

She was silent a moment. "Alara."

"Beautiful," he murmured. "And unique. Wasn't that the name of the first High Queen?"

Her delicate jaw ticked. "Yes."

He grinned. "Your parents have a thing for royalty, I take it?"

For at least the third time tonight, she stared at him as if his hair had caught fire.

"Not that there's anything wrong with that," he added hastily. "It's still a very unique name, obsessions and all."

Shit. Just shut your mouth before you ruin this.

Her gray eyes narrowed. "It's not an obsession. It's tradition."

"What, naming you after your mommy and daddy's icons?"

She started to pull away, disgusted, but he held firm. "Hey, I'm sorry, all right? I can be an ass sometimes—okay, most of the time. My brother says I don't know how to filter what comes out of my mouth."

She snorted. "That's an understatement."

He ignored the jab. She was definitely royal—that haughty way she looked at him, like he was street scum, was the same way all the other "elite" looked at lesser-ranked wolves. She was probably some packmaster's daughter. But unlike the others, he found her haughtiness amusing more than irritating. It was cute on her, like she was a softie trying hard to be tough. Besides, it was fun getting a rile out of her. She was so damn sexy when she was irritable.

"I'm not as rough as I seem," he said carefully. "All I'm saying is you don't seem to like your name as much as your parents do. But I don't blame you for getting upset. People tend to wear guises to hide who they really are from the world."

She looked him in the eyes then, like, really looked at him. She looked away, seeming bothered.

Worried that he'd just majorly screwed up made him miss a step. He *never* missed a step. What the hell was wrong with him? He wetted his lips, at a loss for words.

"Did it hurt?"

He looked at her. She was staring at his mouth, and it was giving him dirty ideas. "Does what hurt?"

"Your tongue piercing."

"Oh. That." He flexed his tongue, displaying the silver-colored nub he hadn't taken out. He'd only agreed to remove *most* of his studs. "Nah. Had it a while."

"What on earth would possess someone to poke a hole through their tongue?"

"Haven't you ever done anything on a whim?"

She looked wistful for a moment. He saw the hope,

the longing, in her eyes. Then that sad, resigned shade fell back into place, followed by a composed look she'd probably practiced in the mirror dozens of times to perfect. "Some of us can't afford whims."

"You should try it sometime. Live a little."

"I live enough."

He snorted. "Sure. Doing what, Your Highness? Sewing?"

She stepped on his foot with the heel of her shoe, and he winced slightly.

"Point taken—quite literally. Sorry, that was a sexist blow."

"Ass."

His brows shot up. "Did you just call me an ass? I didn't think ladies swore."

"Who says I'm a lady?" she said in a surprisingly smoky voice.

He slowly smiled. "Are you flirting with me?"

She leaned in, eyes dropping to his lips. "Keep dreaming."

He laughed outright. "Damn! You had me fooled! You're pretty saucy, aren't you?"

She smiled. "I can honestly say that's the first time I've ever been called saucy."

"I could think of a few other adjectives: sexy, confident…." His hand slid lower on her back, his fingers resting along the curve of her bottom. He heard her breath catch as he leaned in, his lips beside her ears. "Beautiful. Captivating."

Her breasts rubbed up and down his chest as her

breathing quickened. He wondered if she could feel him hardening for her. The effect she had on him… he'd never felt anything quite like it before. He could hear her heart beating wildly, could smell the lust seeping out of her. Oh, yes, she wanted him all right. A cherry, waiting to be picked.

And he wanted to have her all to himself.

A man cleared his throat nearby as a figure stepped into their path. Nik had to do some quick maneuvering to keep Alara from slamming into him.

He was about Nik's age and handsome in an old Civil War kind of way. He had a classically straight nose, a muscular frame, and a few scars to his face. Nik instantly gained more respect for him then. He could relate to a fighting man more than these pampered wusses.

The uniformed man bowed low to Alara. "My lady, I was hoping to cut in?"

Nik instinctively growled and pulled her closer. The man's eyes narrowed in warning, a low growl also coming up his throat.

Alara put a hand on both their chests. "Gentlemen, please. Yes, Gerard, I would be delighted." She turned to Nik. "Thank you, Mister…?"

"Nik. Call me Nik." He grabbed her gloved hand and brought it to his lips, kissing it. "The pleasure's been all mine, Lady Alara."

Color rose to her cheeks again. God, she was so pretty when she blushed. Did she have any idea how she was making him feel, of the delicious chaos raging inside him as he gazed at her?

Gerard gave Nik a look that said, "Get lost, Beta scum."

Nik gave him a curt nod, at last tearing his eyes off Alara as he walked away. He couldn't get the feel of her body off his mind. Still, his sex yearned to be inside her, to make sweet love to her like no wolf had ever done before.

He scowled. She was not yet marked. She was royal, and royals, especially of her caliber, almost always marked other royals. He was foolish to think he could bed her so easily.

He smiled to himself. "You silly dreamer."

The thought of her lying in another man's arms, naked, drove him near mad. He went for the bar, ordering a glass of Scotch. As he drank, he couldn't take his eyes off the dancers, his gaze furtively searching for the woman who'd so captivated him.

He caught them waltzing closer to the door—and she was looking his way.

Alara.

Gerard followed her gaze, his eyes landing on Nik, to which Nik grinned and waved.

Gerard promptly looked away, his form noticeably stiffer than before.

Nik snickered.

"You're awfully chipper. What's put you in such a good mood?"

Nik didn't turn at his brother's voice as he joined him. "Eh. I'm sporting a pretty good buzz. Where's your mate?"

Gage pointed to the dance floor, where an elderly man was spinning her about while she laughed. Gage's eyes got that soft twinkle they always did when he was watching her. Nik knew his brother hadn't taken his eyes off her the entire time. He was very protective of his mate, as all werewolves were, but especially since she almost died.

"It looked like you were getting close to the brunette over there."

Nik shrugged. His temperature flushed as he remembered the feel of her curves beneath his palm as it glided over the silk. He could feel himself getting hard again just thinking about it.

"You do realize who that is, don't you?"

"What do you mean? She's some lord's daughter. Her manners are evidence enough of that." Nik took a sip of his champagne.

"Oh, she's some lord's daughter all right. That's Alara Crescent, daughter of High King Victor Crescent."

Nik spit out his drink. "You're shitting me."

"I shit you not."

Nik looked back at Alara as she danced. So his hunches were right—she *was* royal. He just hadn't expected her to be high royalty, as in, future High Queen of their kind. All his flirting and hopeful puppy dog eyes…. He'd been screwed before he'd even had a chance. Princesses didn't mark nobodies.

He became aware Gage was watching him carefully. Shit. He was getting careless. He had to keep up his cover. His little brother had enough on his mind. With a wide grin, he said, "So how's the party?"

"Dull, but I knew it would be," Gage said. His tone turned serious. "I may have a lead on Mistress Black."

Nik immediately straightened. "What do you know?"

"Nothing yet. But one of the werewolves sought me out and said he might have something."

"Point him out to me."

Gage turned around and discreetly whispered, "The blond-haired gentleman across the room, talking to the Davenport Alpha and his mate."

Nik's eyes met an older man's from across the room. The silver flower pin shone from his lapel. "That's our informant?" he hissed. "He's a Nightshade."

"I know."

Nik studied Gage. "Do you trust him?"

"What choice do I have? No one's been able to dig up anything on Mistress Black. I can't risk my mate's—or my pack's—safety. I have to do whatever it takes to find out who she is."

Nik hated the desperation in his brother's voice. Not that he'd know anything about mates, but Nik was dead certain if someone had tried to kill his little brother—someone he loved more than anyone else in the world—he would do anything necessary to track down the assassin. Nik downed the rest of his champagne. "I'll go with you."

They started to walk over to the other side of the room when gunfire broke out. Nik immediately grabbed Gage and hit the floor as Gage cried out his mate's name.

"Danica," he said frantically.

"I know," Nik replied. "We'll find her."

More gunfire—there were multiple assailants. Nik couldn't risk his brother's safety. He listened for the source of the assault.

It was coming from the ballroom.

His heart skipped a beat in fear.

"Alara."

CHAPTER FOUR

T FIRST, ALARA DIDN'T BELIEVE WHAT SHE WAS hearing. There couldn't possibly be gunfire, but it sure sounded like it, coming from multiple directions. Then there was the sensation of something grazing her arm, right before Gerard slammed her into the floor and shielded her with his own body.

"Attack!" he bellowed. "Guards, get the high family out of here!"

Alara looked around frantically as people screamed and scrambled about. It was total chaos. She wasn't even sure what she was searching for until Gerard hauled her up and started ushering her to a side door.

"Alara!"

She inwardly breathed a sigh of relief as Nik came running toward her, though she had no idea why. With his piercings and tattoos, he looked more likely to be the shooter than her savior. Despite all that, she found the outward display of rebellion oddly enticing. Which was unusual, because the captain was generally more her type. Clean-cut. Well-mannered.

Safe.

She blinked several times. What the hell was wrong with her? She'd just been shot, and here she was weighing the physical pros and cons of the men around her.

His eyes immediately snapped onto her arm. "You're bleeding."

"It's nothing," she said.

"Get out of my way, Beta," Gerard growled.

Without asking for permission, Nik swept Alara up into his arms, clean out of Gerard's grasp. She felt her cheeks heat as he cradled her body to him, holding her as if she weighed no more than a feather. It felt... good. Right, even.

Gerard stood there, mouth open in outrage. "What the hell do you think you're doing?"

"Getting her out of here. You should see to your guards, *Captain*." Nik hurried to the exit. No sooner had he taken a step when his fingers brushed her bare skin, and light shone through the lace of her glove. She ripped it off. A bright blue glow filled the space around them, coming from the back of her hand.

It didn't hit her at first what was happening. But as the light dimmed, shimmering along her skin in the form of a pretty, swirling powder-blue symbol, she knew what had just happened. She stared at her hand. "You marked me." It sounded insane coming out of her mouth, but saying it aloud made it no less true.

She didn't know how to name the look in Nik's eyes. He seemed more afraid now than when they were being shot at. Finally, he blinked, composing himself. "So it appears," he said quietly.

She stared at him. "This has to be a mistake. You're not royal."

The briefest flickering of hurt flashed through his eyes, and she bit her tongue, suddenly sorry to have sounded so arrogant. Since when did she care so much about bloodlines? Maybe her mother and father had rubbed off more on her than she at first thought.

"The Mark never lies, love," Nik said grimly, walking through the hall past frightened guests. People shoved past them, in a hurry to get out, but they were moving in the opposite direction.

She shoved the troubling—and appetizing—idea of being mated to Nik out of her mind for now. "Um, shouldn't we be following the crowd?"

"Oh, sure. Put us all in one place to make us easier to shoot. No, thanks. If that's your captain's idea of safety, then he's an idiot."

She bristled. "He's one of the most brilliant knights to be inducted into the Order of the Moon."

"And he has the hair product to prove it, too, I bet."

She made a fist and hit him, wincing when her thumb popped.

"Tuck your thumb on the outside, not in," Nik said with a smile. "That's a good way to break it with the way you have it."

"Shut it," she growled.

The gunfire had stopped, but Nik never slowed his pace. Alara could hear Gerard barking orders from the foyer. "One of the assailants has been killed," she said, listening in.

"Exactly—*one* of them. Until I know how many there are, we're staying hidden. This is as good a place as any."

He kicked open a door and barged in, shutting and locking it behind him. It was one of the sitting rooms her father used to entertain guests. Windows covered by pulled drapes lined one wall, and expensive sofas and chairs sat about the floor.

"Plenty of exits," Nik said, eyeing the windows approvingly. "In any case, we should stay down. Wouldn't want to go to all this trouble and then get nicked by a stray bullet if they start shooting again." Nik pulled her to the floor, keeping an arm around her. She had the mind to feel outraged he would dare pull a princess so close. She might have even considered slapping him—if, that is, she didn't like the feel of his hand on her waist so much.

Her brain warred with her hormones. *It's the Fever, that's it. No way would you be attracted to someone so rough-looking, so rude... so deliciously handsome and brave.*

She shook her head and blushed when she realized Nik was watching her with an amused gleam in his eyes.

"You all right?" he asked.

"Fine. Just dizzy from the adrenaline rush," she said, mentally wincing at how breathy her voice sounded.

He looked at her arm, which had stopped bleeding. "Does it hurt?"

"To move it? Yes. It'll be sore, but the bullet just grazed me. It didn't go in." The wound had already closed up thanks to her accelerated healing. A few more minutes and it would be nothing more than a faded scar.

"Thank God," Nik murmured, pulling her closer.

Her heart began to pound. She could smell the cologne he was wearing, a dark, musky scent that reminded her of sin. Beneath the silk of her dress, her nipples tightened, and she felt a pull deep below her navel, a longing to join with her mate forever.

She had heard the mating Fever was insane. Most of the time the mates were strangers, then BAM! They got hit with crazy lust and couldn't take their eyes—or their paws—off one another. It sounded so ludicrous. Never in her life had she wanted to bed a complete stranger. It wasn't something a lady would do.

Until now.

"You're breathing heavier," Nik said huskily, running his thumb up and down her spine.

She swallowed hard. "Am I?"

He leaned in closer, and she forgot how to breathe. "Do I frighten you, my lady?"

His lips were beside her jaw. She sighed, leaning into him as he drew his arm tighter around her. "No."

"Do I…." He slowly kissed her jawline, sending exquisite shivers tingling across her skin. "Entice you?"

She dug her nails into his arms. "Yes."

With his free hand, he tenderly stroked her cheek, then let his fingers trail down her breasts to finger the tight, round nipple of her right breast through the soft silk. She sighed, throwing her head back and rubbed her aching breasts against his hand, whimpering as he toyed with her nipples in slow, tantalizing movements.

"Oh, Alara," he breathed, his voice more ragged than before. "Do you have any idea what you're doing to me?"

She had a pretty good image in mind. She felt like she was going crazy inside, like all this restless energy was building up and craving a release. She wanted to rip his pants off, mount him, and ride him until she screamed.

Slowly, he trailed kisses down her neck, kissing the crown of her breasts. She sighed with longing, gripping his back and pulling him closer as he peeled back the fabric at the top of the dress.

He paused, his breath coming hard and hot against her skin.

She opened her eyes. She didn't even know she had closed them, she was so taken with him. "What's wrong?"

A stricken look flickered over his features. Clearing his throat, he straightened her dress and sat up, looking away.

She studied him, ducking her head to try to see his face. "Nik?"

His Adam's apple bobbed as he swallowed. "It's nothing. I'm sorry for getting carried away, my lady. It won't happen again."

Her heart sank. Did she do something wrong? She'd never had a boyfriend before. Her parents would never allow her or her sister to date. What was the point, when you might not end up with them in the first place?

She touched his arm gently. He looked at her then,

eyes searching hers. She wasn't sure what she was seeing there at first. Then it hit her.

Pain.

She knew because it was the same look she saw in her own eyes every time she looked in the mirror.

Nik, what's happened to you?

Someone called her name, running past the door, followed by more shouts.

"They're looking for you," Nik said, rising and adjusting his now rumpled jacket. "We should meet up with the guards. Your parents must be worried sick."

She took his hand and let him pull her up. As soon as she was on her feet, he dropped her hand and turned away. It was like an invisible wall had erected between them. He was distancing himself from her, and she had no idea why.

She started to reach for him, to tell him they could wait, but he was already walking toward the door.

For a moment, she didn't move. She didn't want this moment to end. For a few seconds, she had felt wanted and desired, something that had never happened to her before. Men flirted with her, but she knew it was because they hoped to gain favor with the king. They didn't care about her. But Nik, the way he'd kissed her and touched her, awakening feelings she'd never felt before...

She clenched her thighs, realizing when she shifted her weight that she was wet. It made the heat coursing through her intensify.

Nik turned back to her, one hand on the doorknob. "Coming, Your Highness?"

"Alara."

"What?"

"I want you to call me Alara."

He smiled, but it didn't reach his eyes. "Very well. Alara, are you coming?"

The desire in his eyes was gone. He looked at her with all the interest of her mother—that is, with none. Whatever had happened between them was lost.

With a resigned sigh, she reluctantly followed behind him.

He stayed by her as they walked down the hall. People huddled together in clusters, shaking and talking amongst one another. Guards were everywhere, and debris from the gunfire littered the floor. Holes poked through the walls, allowing one to see clear into the next room.

"What were they after?" she asked, eyes narrowing as she looked at her decimated home.

"Don't know," Nik said grimly. "But it doesn't appear like anyone else is hurt."

She wondered with fear if Izzy was okay.

"Nik!"

They both turned as a handsome Alpha and a beautiful blond-haired woman walked quickly toward them.

"Thank God," Nik said, embracing the man. "I was worried about you. Are you and Danica all right?"

"We're fine," Danica said. Her hair looked a little unkempt, probably from hitting the floor and trying to run like everyone else. All the guests looked a bit harried. Danica looked at Alara and smiled warmly. "Hi," she said, extending her hand, "I'm Danica. And this is my mate, Gage, Nik's brother."

Alara blinked, surprised. No one had ever shaken her hand before. Tentatively, she reached up and took the other woman's hand. "Alara. Pleasure to meet you."

Danica's eyes drifted to her hand, widening. "Oh."

Alara followed her gaze. She'd forgotten to put her glove back on. The Mark shone in the light, shimmering with blue crystals.

Gage's eyes landed on her hand, widening. He looked at Nik, a question on his face.

Nik rubbed the back of his neck, looking troubled. "Yeah. The Mark's mine."

Gage blinked, his mouth opening as if to ask a question, when Gerard said, "Alara!"

She had just enough time to look up when he took her into his arms, holding her tightly. She blinked, startled.

"Thank God you're all right. After that fool took you away, I wasn't sure what had become of you. I thought he had kidnapped you."

Nik growled, his hands fisting at his sides, but Gage held him back.

Alara pushed away from Gerard, stepping back to put some distance between them. He stared at her in puzzlement. "I'm sorry to have worried you," she said quickly and politely. "But Nik took excellent care of me."

"I bet he did," Gerard murmured darkly. He and Nik glared at one another, and Danica wetted her lips, stepping between them.

"I hope you apprehended the people who did this," she said, turning the conversation away from Alara. Alara instantly liked her.

"We killed one of the shooters, but the other two got away," Gerard said, all business. "They were warlocks. And they were using enchanted bullets."

"What?" Nik and Gage said at the same time.

"What kind of enchantment?" Gage asked.

"We're not sure yet," Gerard said, seeming irritated with answering his questions. "We sent the bullets off to be tested."

"Who were they after?" Alara asked.

Gerard's eyes were guarded. "We think it was the high family," he finally answered.

Alara's chest tightened. She didn't like the look on his face. "Was someone injured?" When he didn't answer, she gripped his arms. "Was it Izzy? Please, Gerard, tell me!"

Nik put a hand on the small of her back, letting her know he was there for her. First hot, then cold, now luke-warm. It irritated her. She didn't have time to figure out his mood swings right now, not with the possibility of her sister being dead looming before her.

Gerard took a deep breath, staring at her with regret. "Your sister and father are fine. It's your mother. The queen's been severely wounded."

CHAPTER FIVE

LARA'S EYES WIDENED AS EVERY DROP OF BLOOD drained from her face. "Severely wounded? Where is she? You have to take me to her!"

"Alara," Gerard began, but she jerked out of his grasp.

"No," she said, lifting her chin. "I want to see her—*now*."

Gerard searched her eyes. Nik watched the captain carefully. The captain genuinely cared about Alara—that much was clear. And from the way she looked at him, she obviously cared about him too.

His heart sank.

Gerard at last sighed. "Very well. Come with me."

Alara stepped forward, not even glancing behind her as she walked away. That stung, but Nik told himself he was being selfish. It was her *mother*, for crying out loud. If he were in her shoes, he wouldn't have been able to think about anything else either. Not that he had much to relate to. His parents hadn't exactly been model citizens.

Either way, he couldn't let her out of his sight, not after hearing the shooters had been after the high family. He started to follow when Gage grabbed his arm. "Wait."

Nik turned on his brother, the growl in his throat dying when he saw the question—and the hurt—in his brother's eyes.

He sighed, the fight leaving him. "I can explain."

"You've had the Fever and you didn't tell me." It was almost an accusation. "How long?"

Nik ran a hand along his neck, which had suddenly grown stiff. "About three weeks."

Gage swore. Danica stepped away a few steps, turning her back. Nik knew she could still hear them, with her wolf hearing, but he appreciated the considerate gesture.

"And you didn't think telling me it was your Blood Moon month was important?" Gage said, his words sharp with fury. And hurt.

An answer formed on Nik's tongue, but he paused. *I didn't want to tell you because I didn't want you to push me into something I didn't want. I didn't want to pretend like this is what I want because it's what you want.* Neither of them sounded right. Hurting Gage was the last thing he wanted. He'd been through so much already. So he went with the only one that sounded honest and not hurtful. "I didn't want you to worry about me."

All the anger drained out of Gage, and he sighed. "I'd worry about you anyway. You're my brother." His voice softened. "I noticed something was off, but you always keep everything in, so I thought at first it was my imagination. You don't show your emotions very easily."

"Not like you?" Nik said with a small chuckle.

Gage smiled back. "It's what makes you so good at politics, whether you want to admit it or not."

A sour expression crossed Nik's face. Gage had tried to get him to run for Alpha, but Nik would have no part of that. He might have an excellent poker face, but he still had a temper. Some king would step out of line and get thrown into a wall, and before he knew it, his pack would be in all-out war. It was too big a risk. Gage's personality was much more suited to this job.

Gage stepped closer, studying him with concern. "When did you start hiding things from me again? I thought we were past this."

Nik shrugged, giving his brother that carefree smile. "Old habits die hard, I guess."

Gage shook his head in frustration. "That's just it. You pretend like everything is okay inside when it's not. Just open up to me."

Open up. Nik's pulse quickened with fear. The last time he'd opened up to someone—truly let them see who he was—she'd left him and it nearly destroyed him. He was already raw from trying to win his parents' affections, something that had proved futile when they'd left him too. All his life people had walked out on him. He couldn't take any chances at letting them get too close; otherwise, they'd hurt him when they left.

Gage's voice was gentle, so full of understanding. "I don't need you to treat me like your baby brother anymore. I can help you. Let me look out for you for a change."

Nik looked at his brother, at the kindness and love in

his eyes. His throat tightened with emotion. Mutely, he nodded and Gage embraced him, clapping a hand on his back.

Nik smiled softly at him. "Thanks," he said shakily.

Behind Gage, Danica smiled.

"Are you Nikolas Johnson?"

They both turned to look at the pair of guards who'd sneaked up on them.

Nik raised a brow. "Who wants to know?"

"His Majesty, High King Victor, would like an audience with you."

Shit.

"What's this about?" Gage said with authority, becoming the Alpha of the Moonstruck Pack once more as he stepped forward.

"I think you know very well what this is about," one of them said with a sneer toward Nik.

Nik could take a few guesses. And he bet all of them had to do with Alara. "Right, then. Lead the way."

Gage and Danica followed Nik and the guards up the stairs to the second story and down the hall. Gilt lined the walls, and frescoes stretched across the ceiling in swirling patterns of the heavens. Nik would have taken more time to admire the artwork if his heart wasn't beating faster with every step they took as they neared the king's office.

More guards waited outside the room. They opened the doors and announced Nik. Nik glanced at Gage, who gave him an encouraging nod, as if to say, "I've got your back." He started to follow Nik in when the guards crisscrossed their swords. "Only Nikolas may enter. The king has not called for you."

Gage growled and opened his mouth to protest when Nik cut him off.

"It's okay," he said quickly. "I'll be fine." *I don't want to cause any more trouble than I'm already in*, he added telepathically.

Gage gave him a look that said he still wasn't okay with this, but he stood down. *Let me know if you need me, and I'm there.*

Nik smiled. *Thanks.*

The first thing Nik did when he walked in was glance around—first, for exits, and secondly, for—

"She's not here," said the king. He sat behind his desk, head leaned forward and pinching the bridge of his nose.

Nik raised a brow and bowed. "Your Highness."

The king chuckled, low and bitter. "I never thought I'd live the day to see my queen dying and the heir to my throne mark a peasant."

Nik nearly snorted. Kings loved to throw around those words. He thought they did so because it assured them of their own self-importance.

The king stood, drawing himself up to his full height. Nik felt the force of the hatred in his eyes. "I'm not all right with this," he said. "As this has to be some mistake, I will hire the best witches and warlocks available and have them remove the link between you two so my daughter may mate with someone within her own class."

Nik blinked, then crossed his arms. "The Mark can't be undone."

"There are always loopholes in spells," the king said

dismissively, sitting down. "I'll find a way. This union cannot happen."

Nik's heart skipped a beat. At first, he was terrified at growing closer to her, but he found he was more afraid of losing her.

The king went on before Nik could think to speak. "For their protection, my daughters are being moved to our other strongholds. After that, you will never see her again."

Now Nik's anger boiled over. "She's coming with me," he said with quiet fury.

The king scoffed. "Don't be ridiculous. I know you only fancy yourself a knight of hers after marking her—"

"Oh, I don't just fancy myself her knight—I am her mate." His voice grew with strength. "She is my Marked. You cannot fight that."

"I can and I will," the king said, voice hard as stone. "Look, if it's a title or money you seek—"

"I don't want your damn money," Nik snapped. "And I sure as hell never asked to be some fancy-pants royal."

"Then why do you want her? You can't say you possibly care for her."

Nik wasn't sure if the derision in the king's voice was aimed at him or Alara. The latter nearly sent him into a rage. He hadn't known Alara long, but the Fever amplified his feelings, making them irrational. And they made him want to protect her all the more. He remembered seeing her face when he teased her about her name, the resentment in her eyes. Anger like that was hard to hide, the kind that could only be built up after years and years of conditioning. She was as much a prisoner here as she was a princess. He had to save her. "What if I do?"

"It's of no consequence to me. You will not mate with my daughter!" the king said, rising and slamming a fist down on the desk.

Nik never backed down from his icy gaze. "Fight it all you want. But either way, she's my mate and she's coming with me."

Without another word, he turned his back and stormed out on the High King.

Gage fell into step beside him once he started walking down the hall. *Did you just...?*

Yes. That was me, walking out on the High King.

Damn. This is doing nothing to improve relations between us and them.

I don't care. He's threatening to take Alara away from me.

What are you going to do?

Nik's eyes narrowed. It was "game on" time. *Find Jason. I have a plan.*

CHAPTER SIX

ALARA SQUEEZED HER MOTHER'S CLAMMY HAND, HER heart constricting. It sounded cruel, but sometimes she'd fantasized about her mother dying. If she wasn't around, she wouldn't be able to needle Alara over how inadequate an heir she was.

But seeing her lying on her bed, her face devoid of color and her breathing so shallow, Alara couldn't get the taste of fear out of her mouth.

Izzy sat on the opposite side of the bed, holding their mother's other hand. The lighting had been kept low on purpose, since their mother had complained about it. Only a few candles lit the room, making it gloomier than ever. Even the shadows seemed thicker.

Alara worried her lip, unable to remove her eyes off their mother's fevered face. She'd been shot in the shoulder—the killer had narrowly missed her heart. High werewolves kept a Blue Witch—skilled in the art of healing, as well as water—around in case of emergencies. She said the wound might not have been as bad had the bullets not been silver. The toxins had gotten into the queen's bloodstream, meaning the witch had to use a more complicated spell to heal her. Plus, there was an enchantment coating the bullet which made the silver liquefy and spread. Because of that alone, it took twice as long to heal the queen. It also took more out of both the witch and the werewolf. The queen had lost a lot of blood while the bullet was being extracted. The witch said she'd recover, but she would need a lot of rest. That was why she'd brewed a potion to help her sleep. With her shoulders worked into knots and her nerves fried, Alara might have to hit her up for some sleeping potions herself later, like some magical Nyquil.

Their mother hadn't opened her eyes, but she kept muttering to herself and her head jerked about the sweat-soaked pillow.

"What is she saying?" Izzy said quietly, eyeing Alara from across the bed.

"I don't know." Alara frowned. "It almost sounds like a name. Maybe she's dreaming?"

"Ste… fan."

They both looked up in bewilderment, then at each other. "Who's Stefan?" Izzy whispered.

Alara shrugged, frowning. She remembered sneaking a peek at a letter her mother was working on when she was little. It had been sitting on her dresser. The queen had gotten upset while she was writing it. Alara had tried to comfort her, but the queen had only pushed her away, growing more distant than she already was when all five-year-old

Alara wanted was to be a part of her life.

Alara shook her head to rid her thoughts of the troubling memory. Her affection waned for her mother. Standing, she started to let go of her mother's hand when the queen's fingers suddenly tightened. "I want… my daughter," she rasped.

Alara squeezed back, her heart soaring. She sat down and brushed back some wisps of hair from her mother's face. "I'm right here, Mother."

The queen's eyes cracked open slightly, and she squinted. A look of confusion came over her face, and she shook her head. "My other daughter."

Alara went cold all over. The queen might as well have slapped her. She went still, and Izzy bit her lip, frantic eyes drilling a hole into Alara's head.

Mouth pressed into a thin line, Alara stood and started toward the door.

"Alara—" Izzy started.

"I need some air," Alara said, cutting her off. She closed the door behind her and walked briskly toward the balcony on the second landing. With every step, it became harder and harder to suppress the tears building in her eyes.

Guards stood near the balcony, blocking her path. "King's orders. No one leaves."

Alara stormed past them. "If you're so worried, then come with me," she growled. At this point, she didn't care if someone put a bullet through her heart. It was already broken to begin with.

At a loss, the guards looked at each other and followed

her outside.

Darkness had started to fall, cloaking everything in shades of blue. Stars twinkled above, and the moon tried peeking out behind a patch of cloud cover.

The first thing she did was stomp over to the balcony, ball up her fists, and hit the railing as hard as she could. Her knuckles popped, but it felt good. She might go down to the gym later to take out her frustrations on the punching bag.

Silently, she bit her lip to keep the sobs from escaping as tears ran down her face. She kept her back to the guards, and they didn't make any moves to bring her back inside. That is, until Gerard showed up.

"What's going on?" he asked, strolling onto the balcony. "I didn't authorize this!"

The guards shifted their weight. "We're sorry, sir. She ordered us to let her through."

"And you actually listened?" he snapped. He sighed in exasperation, closed his eyes, and pinched the bridge of his nose, muttering about "the help being useless." He turned to Alara, who had hastily patted her face dry while he wasn't looking. "Come, Lady Alara, let's get you back inside."

She ducked her head to hide her gaze. "I'm not going," she said in a low voice.

He hesitated, his hand pausing midair while reaching for her. "Come again?"

"I said"—she raised her head, her voice rising in volume—"I'm not going!"

His mouth dropped open as shock spread over his

face. She'd never raised her voice to him, ever. He fumbled for words. "Alara...."

The gentleness he spoke her name with made her emotional walls crack all over again. Tears fell down her face, faster and faster, as she held Gerard's gaze. In one step he had closed the distance between them and taken her in his arms, holding her as she cried onto his shoulder.

He didn't say anything as her shoulders shook with silent sobs.

"It's all right," he murmured, stroking her hair soothingly. "No one will hurt you."

"I know," she hiccupped, and she believed him. He would die before letting anything happen to her—literally. All knights had to swear an oath to the royal line, part of which meant giving their lives for the crown if necessary. And here she was, standing on the balcony out in the open, when there could still very well be a threat lurking in the shadows below. How selfish could she be?

She pulled away and composed herself. "I'm all right. Just stressed."

Gerard tenderly brushed away tears from her cheeks, cupping her face in the palms of his hands for a moment. "You know I would do anything for you, and you can tell me anything, right?" he said, a sad look on his face.

"I know." She sniffed. But she wouldn't tell him. She wasn't ready to admit out loud yet that her mother loved Izzy way more than she loved her. Somewhere inside the adult who didn't care was a child who yearned to be accepted and loved by her mother. Was she not as important as Izzy? Was she not as special and deserving of her mother's love?

Numb, she whispered to herself.

With practiced ease, she took a deep breath and let the calmness spread through her. She stepped back from Gerard. "I'm fine," she said, deadpan. "I just needed some fresh air."

He made a frustrated grunt. Apparently, that hadn't been the response he'd been hoping for. Letting his hand drop away, he returned to being the soldier once more. "I will give you another few minutes to compose yourself, my lady. Please, for your own safety, return to your rooms."

With that, he turned and strode away without a backwards glance.

She watched him leave, then turned and looked over the grounds. The garden lights twinkled below, lighting up the pathways with orange and red light. Normally, when she was stressed, she would take a stroll through her mother's garden, but therein lied the problem—it was her *mother's* garden. She couldn't possibly walk there right now because it would remind her too much of her and all that had happened tonight. Besides, she knew Gerard wouldn't allow her to walk in the garden, even with escorts. The more she stared out at the open space, the more she felt like the castle walls were closing in on her, suffocating her. She yearned to escape, to be truly free. For a moment, she allowed herself to fantasize about running away with Nik.

She stared at the glimmering Mark on her hand. Would it be so bad to be his mate? She liked the way he held her, the way he made her feel. He treated her like an

equal, not his superior. He drove her mad with his attitude, but she hadn't exactly been very polite to him the
first time they'd met either.

Almost as an afterthought, she touched her lips. What
would it be like to kiss him, to share herself with him as
she'd done with no other man? Her cheeks burned as she
felt a deep wave of desire roll through her.

Her father would never allow the match. He would
keep her locked away in a tower and throw away the key
before letting his daughter mate with a commoner.

Defying her father's expectations only made her want
Nik more. She imagined finding him, having him rip
open her dress and make love to her against whatever
surface they had available. Her father wouldn't be able to
do a damn thing after they'd bound themselves together
forever.

She took a deep breath, calming down her raging libi-
do. She couldn't do that to Nik—or to herself. Not that either of them had much of a choice in the matter. It was either mate or be destined never to fall in love. Supposedly,
the spell that caused two wolves to Mark one another
meant they were practically soul mates. But Alara knew all
too well that while "like" could eventually turn into "love,"
"love" could also turn to "hate" just as easily.

With that cheerful thought, she pushed the matter
from her mind before she became any more depressed.
Her hand tightened into a fist. She didn't like leaving
things like this between her and her mother. She knew the
queen was too proud to say anything about it, which meant
Alara had to speak first. She needed to tell her mother how

she'd made her feel, no matter how difficult that might be. Her stomach tingled with nerves and the fear of rejection. What if her mother admitted she didn't want her?

That's a risk you'll just have to take.

Mentally, she braced herself, gathering every ounce of willpower she had. She was so wrapped in her own thoughts she didn't notice she was alone until she turned to walk back inside and didn't see her guards. She paused. "Hello?" she called.

No answer.

Maybe they left with Gerard and I just didn't notice.

Trying not to freak out over nothing, she lifted her skirts and started toward the door when a hand shot out of nowhere and pulled her into the shadows.

CHAPTER SEVEN

Nik pulled Alara against his chest, one hand cupped across her mouth. "Sssh, it's me."

She instantly stilled. Soon as she stopped struggling, he let go, and she whirled on him. She shoved him, fury on her face. It looked more cute rather than intimidating.

"You scared me to death!"

"Looks like you're still breathing to me."

"You know what I mean. What are you doing? Where are my guards?"

"Sleeping off the hard knocks I gave them," Nik replied smoothly, crossing his arms in a dare, as if to say, "What are you going to do about it?"

Her jaw dropped. "You knocked out my guards? Why?"

"They were in the way." He shrugged. "I needed to speak with you alone and make sure no one saw us."

Her eyes narrowed. "Why?"

Nik swallowed hard, suddenly nervous. "I spoke with your father. He knows about us."

She paled slightly. "Oh."

"It wasn't pretty."

"I imagine not, knowing Father. What did he say?"

"Oh, the usual things I hear from fathers. 'You're not good enough for my daughter.' 'Stay away from my daughter.' You know."

She grimaced. "Sorry."

"Nothing to apologize for." He brushed a curl away from her cheek, enjoying how her pale skin flushed at his touch. He briefly allowed himself to dream what that lovely flush would look like on the rest of her body as he ravished her.

"Nik?"

He blinked, snapping out of his fantasy. "Sorry. Got distracted." He took her hands, staring into her eyes. "He says he's moving you and your sister for your own protection. He means to separate us for good. I want you to come with me."

"What?" She blinked several times, startled. "Go with you where?"

"I don't know. We can't go back to Crescent Manor, my pack's place. That's the first place they'll look. Gage figured we shouldn't tell anyone where we were going to help hide our trail. We'll just hit the open road and find someplace secluded to hide out in."

He could feel her heart rate pick up as she deliberated. "What about my sister? My mother?"

"We'll come back to them, eventually," he said. "You're

not leaving forever. I'm just afraid if he takes you from me, I'll never see you again." His voice lifted on the last word, and she nodded gravely.

"And we'll both be doomed to the curse, never able to fall in love." She sounded doubtful, like she didn't fully believe that was possible. Or maybe she was a pessimist like him and already thought she couldn't fall in love.

When Alara didn't say anything, he began to panic. "I won't force you to go," Nik said, squeezing her hands. "But I won't leave you, either. I'll stay and fight." He had no idea where those words had come from. When he first marked her, he had planned on just leaving her behind. The curse would be almost welcome. If he couldn't fall in love, he couldn't get hurt. But the thought of never seeing her again made his blood turn to ice and his inner wolf howl in mourning.

Damn this Fever!

When she looked at him, the sorrow in her eyes made him tense. She was going to turn him down. He would have to stay, possibly be killed, knowing the king's ruthlessness. No matter. If staying and fighting was in his cards in order to be near her, then so—

"I'll go."

His breath caught. "You will?"

She nodded, an excited sparkle coming over her eyes. "When do we leave?"

"My, my, anxious to run away with me, are you?" he murmured.

She looked down, pressing her lips together as her cheeks reddened.

He smiled. "We leave now." Scooping her up into his arms, she gave him a surprised look as he climbed up on the edge of the balcony. "Hold on."

She sucked in a breath and wrapped her arms around his neck as he jumped. They dropped into the shadows, landing with a soft thump. What would injure a normal man was nothing for a werewolf.

Setting her down, he took her hand and walked along the side of the building. Guards patrolled out front, all armed. Nik counted six. *There will be more along the sides*, Alara said through their newborn mate-bond. *Gerard likes to keep at least twenty guards around the perimeter at all times; ten by the house, and ten on the grounds and along the driveway.*

Nik grinned, adrenaline making his pulse race. *Sounds like fun.*

Are you always like this?

Only on my good days, sweetheart.

She rolled her eyes. *So how exactly are we going to get out of here?*

No sooner had she spoken than howls ripped through the woods at the front of the property. The guards were on high alert instantly. Silently, they began to reform, the guards at the house taking up defensive positions while the outer guards were drawn away.

"Now's our chance," Nik said, taking Alara's hand. "Get ready to run."

Shouts rang from the woods, followed by gunfire. Nik's gut twisted. He hoped his brother knew what he was doing. Nik was more of the "plow or punch through anything standing in the way" approach, while his brother favored sneakier tactics. Such as distractions.

He just hoped he didn't get shot in the process.

Nik, came Jason's voice in his head. Gage had tracked him down earlier shortly after Nik had walked out on the High King. No were could ignore a summons by his Alpha. He had no idea what the pup had been up to, but he was glad to hear his voice.

Where are you? Nik answered back, gripping Alara's hand tighter. Her palm had begun to sweat. It made him nervous. He could easily lose his grip on her. No matter. He would pick her up and carry her if he had to. *Are you close?*

Coming up on the left... with backup.

Backup?

An engine growled and then a black Mustang slid around the driveway, spewing gravel everywhere as the driver swerved to miss the guards. They ducked out of the way as the car blew past, slowing as Nik ran out with Alara in tow. The car screeched to a halt, and Jason reached across the passenger side and opened the door.

"Get in!" Nik shouted, shoving Alara toward the door.

She refused to let go of his hand. "What about you?"

"I'll be right behind you. Just let me bid our hosts good-bye." Turning, he met the guards head-on as they rushed the car. They might have been armed, but it didn't matter against Nik's brute strength. Gage always told him he should have been a professional fighter. When you fend for yourself on the streets in some of the roughest cities in the world, you pick up a thing or two about surviving. Nik was just as much an animal in human form as wolf. By the time it was all said and done, few shots had been fired and no less than six guards lay on the ground, unconscious.

Nik grinned, cracking his knuckles as he got in the front seat of the car. "Never stood a chance."

Jason stared at him, mouth gaping open. "Remind me never to piss you off." He threw the gear into drive and floored the pedal. The tires spun a few seconds, then found traction and the car shot forward.

Danica smiled at Nik from the backseat, where she was seated by Alara. "You two all right?" he asked, giving them both a quick scan.

"We're fine," Danica replied, though her brow creased with worry.

Nik smiled at her. "Don't worry. Gage is one of the fastest wolves I know. He's agile. He'll be fine."

She crossed her arms, a scowl on her pretty face. "That's not what I'm worried about."

Nik raised a brow, and Jason sank a little farther in his seat.

Nik looked at the younger were, noticing the tip of a tattoo above his collar. He pulled the cuff back, exposing the swirling blue tattoo made up of moons and clouds running down his skin. "Jesus," Nik said, "you *mated*? When the hell did that happen?"

"Ask him with whom?" Danica muttered and Jason's eyes widened.

"Shut up!" he hissed.

Nik frowned. For the tattoo to appear, there had to have been witnesses. "Who is it, Jason? Spit it out. And why the hell aren't we stopping to pick up my brother?" He was growing more anxious—and irritable—by the minute.

"There's kind of been a change in plans," Jason began.

"What?" Nik said stonily. "No one told me of this."

"You were kind of busy playing 'knight-in-shining-armor.'"

Nik grabbed a fistful of Jason's shirt, making him jerk the wheel. "Where the hell is Gage?"

"Fine! Take it easy! My mate's coming with a backup car. She'll grab him."

"And who is this mate? How do we know we can trust her?"

"Hey!" Jason shouted angrily. "Don't talk about Shawna like that!"

Nik sat back, stunned. It took a few moments for what Jason had said to sink in. "You—what—with *her*?"

"Yeah?" Jason drawled. "So what? Is there a problem?"

"She's a living mattress."

"So are you."

Alara cleared her throat, pressing her lips together and glaring out the back window.

Nik groaned. *Can it, kid, before you get me in trouble.*

You started it, he grumbled back.

Nik sank into his seat, massaging his temples. "Just drive. We need to put as much distance between us and this place as possible. It won't take them long to realize we've kidnapped their princess."

CHAPTER EIGHT

THEY DROVE THROUGH THE NIGHT, SWITCHING TO AN SUV at one point and ditching the other cars in a parking lot. Alara had never stolen a car before or broken the law in any way, but that's not what bothered her the most. It was the fact she was stuck in a car with a woman who was obviously one of Nik's one-night stands, all while Jason's proclamation Nik slept around kept replaying in her head. She barely spoke as Shawna prattled on and on about the raunchy, impromptu "mating ceremony" she and Jason had while everyone else had been running away from the shooters. Alara's fist tightened more and more, until her nails dug into her palm.

When Shawna started going on about how Nik couldn't compare to Jason's stamina, Alara snapped. "Just shut the hell up!"

Stunned silence fell over the car as everyone looked at her. Her clenched hands shook in her lap, but she set her jaw and didn't apologize for the outburst.

Shawna was the first to recover. "Hey, where the hell do you get off yelling at me like that? Just because you're high royalty—"

"Drop it, Shawna," Nik growled in warning.

She ignored him, scoffing. "How dare you! You're not my—"

"That's enough, Shawna!" Jason shouted.

That shut her up. The female Alpha's mouth flopped open as she blubbered for a response before closing altogether. Alara looked away and inwardly sighed with relief.

No one spoke the rest of the way. Nik didn't even try to reach out to her telepathically, for which she was grateful. She needed time to digest this new piece of information. She supposed she'd seen him as some sort of dark prince charming. Sure, she had guessed initially upon seeing his appearance that he was a little rough around the edges, but as she started to fall under his spell, she'd hoped deep down he wasn't that type of guy. The kind who bedded any woman he pleased without any attachments.

Was that the kind of deal he was hoping for with her if they mated? Would he have no respect for the bond between them?

By the time they crossed over into Tennessee and pulled up at a motel a few miles off the freeway, she was feeling sick.

Jason and Shawna patrolled the perimeter, trying to pick up on paranormal signatures. When they returned, they only had one paranormal to report and it wasn't all that surprising—a succubus, most likely conducting some soul-sucking business.

"Other than her," Jason reported, "there aren't a whole lot of people here. The place is pretty deserted."

"Good," Gage said, unbuckling his seat belt. "I'll get us rooms. Good thing I brought cash on me."

He went inside with Danica while the rest of them waited in the car. Nik kept glancing sidelong at Alara, but she refused to look at him. She still had no idea what to think of these troubling new stories.

Gage and Danica returned a few minutes later, and everyone got out of the car. Nik caught Alara as she swayed. "I'm fine," she said irritably, snatching her arm out of his grasp. "Just hungry."

"Shawna and I will make a food run," Jason said. "I can't imagine a place like this having much more than a vending machine with out-of-date snacks."

"Here." Gage handed him some more cash. "I don't want anyone using credit or debit cards in case the king can trace them."

Jason nodded, and he and Shawna took off.

Nik tried guiding Alara toward the door, but she stepped out of his reach. "I can walk just fine."

He muttered something in exasperation under his breath, and Danica glanced at her with worry.

The motel lobby was small with faded furniture from the sixties. The front clerk let them know there was complimentary breakfast served at six a.m. and there was also a pool. Alara didn't know if she dared visit it, but swimming had always been one of her favorite physical activities. She used to swim laps around their pool to help her think. She'd already made up her mind to go for a swim by the time she reached her room.

Nik walked in behind her.

She stared at him. "What do you think you're doing?"

"Looks like I'm settling in for the night," he said, sitting on the bed and lying back. He tucked his hands behind his head.

Alara shifted her weight, unsure what to say. "There's only one bed in here."

"Then at least it will be warm and cozy," he said with a sexy grin that made her flush. He sighed. "I suppose I can sleep on the floor."

"That's fine," she mumbled. "You don't have to sleep on the floor."

"Do you want to spoon?" he said with a wide grin.

She glared at him. "No." Turning on her heel, she stalked out of the room. Her heart pounded as dizziness hit her. She probably shouldn't swim on an empty stomach, but she wanted desperately to get in the water.

Setting off on her own, she found the indoor pool. There wasn't anyone around, and it was surprisingly clean. She'd half-expected from the run-down exterior to find syringes floating in the water. A sign on the wall read SWIM AT YOUR OWN RISK. NO LIFEGUARD ON DUTY.

Suits me just fine, thank you. She'd been hoping for some privacy.

Taking off her heels, she dipped her toes in. The water was warm. She smiled. Normally, she didn't like heated pools. She much preferred the shock of cool water. But tonight, it seemed relaxing.

I'll just float and take it easy, she told herself as she slipped out of her dress and undergarments. Climbing down the ladder, she kept to the shallow end in case she felt sick again. She floated through the water, relishing the weightlessness. A wild thrill went through her at swimming naked. She was generally a "good girl." She never broke the rules. Never crossed the line. But tonight, hearing her mother wishing for Izzy, the "perfect" daughter, made something inside her snap. That carefully laid mask had cracked, revealing the rebel within. She was weary of conforming to society's expectations. When was she going to live up to her own ideals?

She sighed, feeling her body starting to relax. This was exactly what she'd needed. No drama, no frowning royals, no—

Splash!

Her eyes flew open to find Nik swimming toward her. And he was naked.

She bolted upright and covered her chest with her arms. "How dare you! Get out of here!"

"I'm sorry," Nik said, looking around. "Is this a private pool?"

Her face flamed. "No. I'm naked," she mumbled. *Dammit, stop sounding so breathless!*

He grinned. "What a coincidence. So am I." He swam closer.

She backed away, cursing how the water wouldn't let her move fast enough. "Careful. I bite."

"Kinky." He was directly in front of her now. She dared glance down.

Oh. Oh, my.

He made no effort to hide the erection proudly pointing toward her. Her pulse began to throb harder, along with the sudden strong urge to rub herself up against him, maybe even let him slide inside.

"You look distracted," he murmured, swimming around her.

She swallowed hard, blinking several times. "It's just, I've never swam with a naked man before."

"Something tells me you haven't seen a naked man before."

She whirled on him in outrage. "I have too!"

That amused smile pulled at his lips, like he was trying not to act like everything out of her mouth was funny. "I didn't know princesses were even allowed to date."

"There's always porn. For all you know, I could have a secret stash."

He laughed outright. "A girl after my own heart."

The smile fell off her face at the thought of him ogling other women. That heavy feeling she'd felt earlier in the car returned.

"Hey," he said, immediately turning serious and gazing at her with concern. "What is it?"

"Nothing."

She started to swim away from him, but he followed. "Tell me," he said gently. "You've had that frown on your face since the car ride."

Had she really? She made a mental note to keep a better rein on her emotions. She didn't know this man. Why did she care whom he'd slept with?

"Does this have to do with what Jason said?"

Her eyes widened slightly before she could think to control her reaction.

He growled a sigh and shook his head. "I'm going to kill him," he muttered.

"So it's true then." Her voice was quiet, resigned. Of course a guy like him would have lots of bedmates. Anything that wickedly gorgeous couldn't possibly be a saint.

She'd stopped swimming. Nik stopped in front of her, his warm breath caressing her cheek. His voice was rough as he spoke. "I'm not going to deny what I've done," he said. He tilted her chin up so she'd look him in the eyes. "But I can promise you if you choose me, I'll never look at another woman again."

Her heart started to race. Her throat had suddenly gone dry, making her voice crack. "And why should I choose you?"

He grinned, leaning in and staring at her lips. "Because you think I'm sexy."

"I do not." Her breath was coming in heavier.

"I did rescue you."

"That's beside the point. 'Kidnapped me' is more like it."

He chuckled. His mouth hovered right over hers. "You didn't try to stop me."

She held her breath. Her heart pounded so hard she could feel it in her eardrums. "I didn't want to."

The next second, his mouth was on hers in a blistering kiss. His tongue forced her lips apart, searching out hers.

She moaned as he gripped her waist, pulling her to him. She wrapped her arms around his neck, digging her nails into his back as he hitched her legs around his waist. He walked them over about five feet toward the side of the pool. She barely noticed the movement because he was doing amazing things with his mouth, and she'd never in her life been kissed this way before. It was needy, like he was drowning for her touch. Her back met the wall of the pool, the water all the way up to their shoulders.

Her sex rubbed against his cock, sending warm, tingling sensations cascading through her. She moaned as he bucked his hips, gliding his erection along her sex.

"I want you," he growled as he began kissing her jaw, her neck. "I've wanted you since the first moment I saw you."

Her only answer was a sigh as his lips trailed lower, kissing the crests of her breasts. "You're so beautiful," he breathed, taking one plump breast into his hand and giving it a squeeze. "Every inch of you is flawless."

She almost cried hearing that. She'd been rejected by her family and societal pressures for so long, she'd begun to give up hope she'd find someone who would accept her—even desire her—for the way she was, curves and all.

I will not cry. I will not cry, I will not—

In her effort not to cry, she sniffled. Nik froze, then looked at her face. She ducked her head away, but not before he saw.

"Hey," he said in the gentlest voice she'd ever heard. "What's the matter? What did I do?"

She laughed as he brushed tears from her cheeks with

his thumbs. "Nothing. You're perfect."

"Then what? Tell me? I'll do anything to make it right."

She stared into his eyes. They seemed so earnest, so kind. Why hadn't she seen the kindness there before? Something in her had sensed it, deep down, when they first met. He wouldn't have saved her from that dance, wouldn't have cared if she'd been shot, if he were like the others. He cared about her, not her title. It was damn refreshing.

She smiled, leaning her forehead against hers. "Thank you."

"For what?"

"For seeing *me.*"

He blinked, looking startled at first, then scared. No, not scared—terrified.

Her brows came together. "Nik?"

He cleared his throat, letting go of her. "I'm sorry." He looked at a loss for words, then he mumbled again, "I'm sorry," and turned to leave.

"Wait!" she called out, but he didn't stop.

A moment later, he was gone, leaving her alone in the pool wondering what the hell had just happened.

CHAPTER NINE

NIK'S HEART POUNDED THE WHOLE WAY BACK TO THEIR room. What the hell had come over him? He'd promised himself he wasn't going through this emotional intimacy again, and what had he done? Nearly shagged her in the pool, that's what. And it hadn't just been sex.

He shook his head. *Stupid!*

He felt even worse for just leaving her there without any explanation whatsoever. It wasn't like he was going to pour his heart out or anything. But the way she made him feel, his intense attraction toward her…. It felt dangerous. Being a bit of a danger magnet, he liked it.

Which scared the hell out of him.

Maybe he should let her father try to break the Mark's bind on them. It would be better for Alara if she'd never met him and could go about her life like a normal wolf. Find a nice Alpha to settle down with and rule. And what the hell did Nik know about ruling anyway? Someday,

Alara would be High Queen. Nik was deluding himself if he thought for a second he could become the most powerful were in the nation.

The thought of leaving Alara and never seeing her again made his gut wrench. Could he walk away from her, even if it meant ripping his own heart out?

He'd just gotten the door closed when Alara walked in. "What the hell was that?"

He composed himself quickly and faced her, his poker face once again on. "What was what?"

"You know what I mean." She walked toward him, determined. "One second, you had your tongue down my throat. The next, you act as if it had never happened and ran away with your tail between your legs."

He snorted. "I did *not* run away like a wounded pup."

She crossed her arms. "You sure as hell looked scared."

He raised a brow. "Look at you, swearing. If I didn't know any better, I'd say I'm starting to rub off on you." He let his gaze sweep her body. The satin from the dress was wet, and her nipples stretched against the fabric. "Quite literally, earlier."

"Stop it!" she growled, stomping her foot.

"Stop what?"

"Flirting with me! Making all those empty comments! Look, if you don't have any intention of following through with this, then just leave. I don't play games."

"Neither do I," he said, going perfectly serious. "I wasn't trying to fool you just to get you into bed."

She flushed. He knew for certain now she must be a virgin. Every time he brought up sex, she blushed like a sixteen-year-old school girl. God, when was the last time he'd had a virgin beneath him? The thought of teaching her about all the pleasures of a man's touch made him quiver with desire.

Down boy.

Her bottom lip started to tremble, and he felt like scum. "Come here," he said, starting to take her in his arms.

She resisted and he chuckled. "You don't have to always be so strong around me," he said gently, hugging her anyway.

She pushed against him. "I'm not going to cry on your shoulder, if that's what you're waiting for."

"I know. But I need you to know I'm here for you if you ever need to."

She stilled. When she didn't say anything, he looked down at her. Silent tears were falling down her cheeks.

He held her tighter, a protective urge going through him. Right then, he would have given her the world if he could have.

"Nik?"

He turned to look at her. "Yeah?"

He had no warning before her mouth met his. His eyes widened in shock as she kissed him, wrapping her arms around his neck. It was all he could do to think straight. Before he knew it, he'd picked her up and carried her over to the bed. They crashed atop the cool sheets. He kissed her with equal fervor, deep, scorching kisses that grew the desire in him. She clawed at his shirt as his hands roved all over the wet silk of her ruined dress.

"Fuck it." He sat up and stripped free of the dress shirt. She stared at him in awe, her eyes taking in every inch of his lean, muscular body. They were both breathing hard. Her eyes saddened, and he knew they'd lost the moment. He mentally swore, wishing he'd never stripped.

Her fingertips gently traced the patterns of scars all over his body. "How did you get so many?" she whispered.

His throat tightened, as it always did when talking about his past. "I got in a lot of fights," he said dismissively, laying down beside her with his arms behind his head. He stared up at the ceiling, remembering the pain as teeth, knives, and bullets sliced into his body. Every scar had a story.

"Tell me," she said, resting her head on his shoulder.

He put his arm around her, wanting to keep her close. "How about you change out of that wet silk before you catch a cold?"

"Then you'll tell me?"

He stared at her for a long while. He nodded once and she sat up. When she started to reach for the zipper, he got to it first. "Allow me."

Slowly, he undid the zipper, slipping his hand inside and feeling her soft flesh. She sighed as he kissed the back of her neck, reaching around and squeezing those plump breasts he couldn't get enough of. He let his palm wander down the soft curves on her side as he peeled the dress away, until she was in nothing but her undergarments.

"Take those off, too," he whispered huskily. "I want to see you."

She stiffened.

"What's wrong?" he asked, gently brushing her wet curls away from her shoulder. He liked the look of the curve where her neck rounded out into her shoulder. All her curves were feminine and sexy as hell to him.

"It's just," she finally said, "no one's ever seen me...."

He rested his head against hers so his mouth was beside her ear. "Then let me be the first and the last." He meant it, too. Against his wishes, he was smitten. It was more than just the Fever—he wasn't a fool. Somewhere along the way, she had hooked him.

She slowly stood and turned to face him. Holding his gaze, she reached behind her and unclasped her strapless bra. It fell away, revealing round, full breasts with dark cherry nubs that tightened as the chilly air hit them. Next, she stepped out of her underwear. A soft patch of black hair crowned her, and he felt himself harden. He stared at her, his throat going dry.

She shifted her weight. "Sorry I'm not skinnier."

He held up a hand. "Don't ever undermine yourself, my lady. You are perfect just the way you are."

Tears shone in her eyes again, and her lips parted, like she was at a loss for words.

He stood and reached for his pants zipper. "It's only fair," he said with a wicked grin. He undid the zipper and his pants fell away, followed by his boxers.

She stared at his erection, licked her lips. Her fingertips subconsciously wandered over to her sex and rubbed it. Her chest rose and fell quicker as her breathing grew heavier.

"Do you want to touch it?" he said roughly.

She nodded, eyes still glued to it.

He laid back down and reached for her. She took his hand and he pulled her close. Gently, he guided her hand down to his sex. "Grab it," he commanded.

She wrapped her fingers around his hard length.

"Stroke me."

She stared at his mouth, starting to pump him in smooth, long strokes. He closed his eyes and groaned deep within his throat, bucking his hips with her rhythm. She gasped when his fingers found her crease, his thumb raking across the swollen nub of her sex. She was so damp. What he wouldn't give to slide himself in her now and make love to her....

"No one's ever touched you here before, have they?"

She swallowed hard and shook her head. "Just me."

"Oh? Do you like to play with yourself?" He caressed her deeper.

Her legs parted as she sighed in pleasure, her own hips starting to buck to the rhythm. "Sometimes."

"Where?"

She closed her eyes, a sexy, devilish smile coming over her pretty lips. "In the bathtub. Or in the shower, mostly."

He brought his mouth just over hers. "I'd like to kiss you down there."

She groaned as he touched her deeper, slipping another finger in as she opened up for him and he cupped her. His thumb ran circles across her sex.

She licked her lips. "Shower first."

He chuckled. "As you wish, my lady. I can always kiss you in the shower."

She smiled. "You were going to tell me about your scars."

"It's a little hard to concentrate while you're touching me."

"Do you want me to stop?"

"No. It feels good. Not as good as being inside you will. I bet you're pretty tight. It'll be hot and wet. I bet you'll fit like a glove."

"I don't know if you can fit."

He chuckled. "Now you're just flattering me."

He withdrew his hand and her eyes flew open. "Why are you stopping?"

"I want you to come with me in you. I want to feel you clenching around me." He licked his fingertips. "Tastes sweet."

"Tease." She lay back and took a deep breath, letting it out slowly. "This is just making me hornier."

"Some think foreplay's just as enjoyable as the real thing."

She shrugged. "Guess I wouldn't know." She took a deep breath, trying to calm down.

"Feel better?" he asked.

"Not really. But I'll manage." She winked at him and settled against him, tracing a fingernail along his chest. "You have a lot of tattoos."

"Helps hide the scars."

"Why do you have so many?"

He was silent a moment, his thoughts filled with memories of blood and violence. "You remember Malachite."

She shivered. "His brutality with the Moonstruck Pack is nothing short of legendary." She looked at him in shock. "You didn't know him, did you?"

Nik's gaze grew cold. "For two freshly-turned pups, it was hard trying to find a pack to take us. I got into a lot of fights, mostly trying to protect Gage until he was old enough and tough enough to look after himself. Moonstruck was the only one to take us in. Fitting in was better than being rogue for a werewolf, plus we didn't know what the hell was happening to us or how the Underworld worked." He closed his eyes, remembering the nights spent in the fight rings, when he'd defend his little brother. Taking his place had cost him, but he would gladly do it a hundred times over if it meant keeping Gage safe. "Most of these scars came from the time spent under Malachite's rule until Gage defeated him and took his place."

Alara was silent, tracing patterns along his skin with her nail. "Though it never came to blows, there was a lot of political fighting in my pack," she said. "High-stakes politics can be brutal. I don't remember my mother being so cruel until later. When I was a little girl, she just seemed sad. She went through a bout of depression. Then she had Izzy, and it was like her whole world was suddenly bathed in sunshine. I tried to hate Izzy for stealing my mother's love—the love she'd never truly showed me—but I couldn't. Izzy became my rock. She was kind and gentle. She's not meant to be a queen."

"That's why you bear the burden, as crown princess. To protect her."

"And I'm the oldest," she said bitterly. "But yes."

Nik looked at the woman in his arms. She had scars, too, he realized. They just weren't visible.

Alara laughed half-heartedly. "It's funny, you know? We were rich, and by all outside appearances, happy. But even if you have everything, you can still be miserable."

Nik stilled. "Do you think you could be happy with me?"

She looked at him, her eyes searching his, as if trying to find an answer there. "I don't know," she answered honestly.

"It's a start." Nik held her closer. "I'll never hurt you. I swear it on my life."

She pressed her finger against his lips. "Don't make me promises. I don't want them. I just want you."

Nik stared at her. Someone must have let her down many times for her not to want promises. He could relate. His father promised to look after them, then he killed himself after he became a werewolf. His mother promised to always be there for him, and she left when things got too rough with their dad. His older brother also said he'd stick around, but he hadn't seen him in years. He hadn't been able to find him, either, and he respected that in a way. Sometimes people didn't want to be found.

"I've always wanted to be someone else," Alara said, staring at his chest. Her marked hand was pressed against his pectoral muscles. "Now that I have the chance to be, I'm scared. I've never fit in with my pack, but I've always been a royal."

Nik caressed her cheek. "Just be Alara. That's all I'll

ever ask or want from you."

She caught his hand, twining her fingers with his. "What if Alara isn't enough?"

Nik smiled. "It is for me."

CHAPTER TEN

THEY'D LAIN LIKE THAT FOR A WHILE, JUST TALKING. Eventually, they both dozed off, but Alara couldn't sleep. Too many things weighed on her mind. She slipped out of bed and found someone had left a change of clothes in the hallway, by the door. There were two outfits, one for Nik and one for her. She blushed, wondering if whoever had dropped them off had swung by earlier when she and Nik were being intimate with one another. Picking up the clothes—and a bag of microwavable food that had been left with the clothes—she carted them inside and changed. She was starving but didn't want to wake Nik. So she took the dinner and bottle of water and went to the dining room.

The TV was on, as were the lights. Alara wondered who could be there at this hour when she rounded the corner and saw Danica sitting at a table alone, eating a bowl of cereal. She looked up as Alara approached and smiled. "Good. I'm glad you saw the clothes."

"So you were the one who dropped them off. Thanks." She popped her food in the microwave and set it for two minutes before sitting down. "I hope we weren't too loud."

Danica raised a brow. "Did something happen?"

Alara flushed. "Er—"

Danica laughed. "It's okay. You don't have to go into details. I totally understand. Besides, it's none of my business."

Alara crossed her arms and looked away, nibbling on her lip. She thought about the upcoming Blood Moon and what that meant for her and Nik. It would be nice to talk to another girl about it, especially someone who had been in the same boat not too long ago. Thing is, she didn't exactly know where to start. She'd never had a close girlfriend before. Izzy was the one who made friends easily, not her.

She studied Danica, trying to decide how to ask what was on her mind. Danica seemed nice enough. She had a kind look to her eyes, just like her sister did. She wrung the hem of her shirt. "How can you know you love him?" she blurted.

"Who? Gage?"

Alara nodded.

Danica sighed. "To be honest, it wasn't love at first, but there was a strong attraction and a rightness in being with him I'd never felt before. For someone who's been alone most of her life, that was enough. It felt wonderful. So I decided to stay and figured love would come later." She smiled. "And it did."

Alara thought about that. She had no idea what being

in love felt like. Did she love Nik? She didn't think so, but she definitely liked him. Okay, well, more than "liked him." The thought of leaving him made her stomach turn.

The microwave chimed and she retrieved her dinner. It was steamed veggies, fruit cocktail, and chicken with some kind of glaze. For a nuked dinner, it didn't taste all that bad. At this time, she was so hungry a granola bar would have been divine.

"You scared about the mating ceremony?" Danica asked after a while.

Alara chewed on her food thoughtfully. "It's just, I've never been that close to anyone before. I mean, other than my sister, Izzy. I don't want to screw it up."

Danica smiled sadly. "I can relate. Well, do you like Nik?"

"Yes!" Alara blurted, then blushed harder.

"That's definitely a start," Danica said with a grin. "I can tell you from personal experience he's a great guy. I mean, I haven't been romantically involved with him or anything," she added quickly. "All that stuff Jason said might be true for the old Nik, but I also know for a fact that his past track record says he'll treat a woman right when he does get in a serious relationship."

So he had been involved with someone before. A wave of jealousy rolled through Alara, which was silly. Of course someone like him had had a girlfriend before. Alara wondered how she compared to her. She bet she was skinnier than her, and beautiful. Alara slumped in her seat, feeling more depressed than ever.

Danica watched her carefully. "We can't help who we

were in our past," she said. "All we can do is try to be the best versions of ourselves now." She rose. "For what it's worth, I hope you make the right decision for you."

She smiled and walked off.

Alara sat there for a moment, mulling everything over. What did she want? Did she even have a clue what the best decision for her was?

She strongly desired Nik. That much she was sure of. But could lust and like eventually evolve into love?

She shook her head. Of course it could. That's how the majority of relationships started. Two strangers meet, are attracted to one another, and sometimes if they spend enough time together, that attraction evolves into love.

The thought of leaving home forever made her a bit homesick. Castle Crescent was all she'd ever known. What if there was something better waiting around the corner, in a room a few doors down the hall? Wouldn't she be a fool to pass that chance up and not see where it led?

There was the risk she and Nik might not fall in love. He might even break her heart, much as she didn't want to admit it. If she stayed with her old pack, though, she was doomed to a life she didn't want. She could end up miserable either way. In each scenario, she was gambling with her heart.

And more cards were stacked in her favor with Nik. She wanted to stay with him; she knew that without really thinking about it. The way he held her, the way he made her feel, as if she was beautiful and invincible…. No one had ever made her feel like that before, not even Izzy. Who wouldn't want to hang on to that?

More importantly, she had to ask herself: Could she walk away from him or her crown? Could she have both? Would Nik want to be king? She needed to talk this through with him.

Finishing off her dinner, she rose from her seat and went back to their room.

CHAPTER ELEVEN

Nik woke up and didn't see Alara. "Alara?" He sat up, looking around. Fear for her made his heart start racing.

You're freaking out over nothing, he assured himself as he got out of bed. *She probably just went to find the snack machine.*

But what if it wasn't nothing? What if something had happened to her? Or worse, what if she'd decided she didn't want to be with him after all and had called up her knight-in-shining-armor Gerard to come get her?

He growled, shaking his head. "Stop being so paranoid," he told himself. "Just go find her, you pussy."

A bag sat on the luggage table. Thank God. Someone had the foresight to bring them clothes. A cheap T-shirt and jeans that were a little snug were inside, along with some clean socks and some knock-off brand sneakers. He didn't care if someone had found them in a Dumpster at this point so long as they were dry and clean.

Nik tugged off his tuxedo pants and dress shirt and dressed in the change of clothes. Not a perfect fit, but whatever. He started to walk out the door when he spied his pack of cigarettes lying on the table. He stared at them, blinking once, then picked them up and stuffed them in his pocket. Surprisingly, he hadn't craved a cigarette since meeting Alara.

He grinned. Maybe she was bringing out the best in him already.

Lacing up and tying his shoes, he went off in search of his mate.

He smiled to himself. *Look at that. You're already thinking of her as your mate.*

He was falling dangerously fast for this woman. He just hoped he didn't crash and burn.

Voices drifted to him from the dining room. He peered around the corner, seeing his Alara sitting there with Danica. The two seemed to be deep in conversation. Not wanting to invade their privacy—because he couldn't stand when people did it to him—he decided to leave them be and seek out Gage.

Where are you?

Gage responded right away. *In my room. Everything all right?*

Yeah. Mind if I stop by?

Sure.

Gage told him his room number, and a moment later, Nik found it and was standing inside his doorway.

Nik paced restlessly. "I'm screwed. It's happening

again."

Gage watched him from the bed with interest, flipping the TV off. "What is? You being an ass again?"

Nik gave him a pointed look. "No. I think I'm falling for her."

"Isn't that a good thing?"

Nik growled a frustrated sigh. "It's not like with you and Danica. You haven't had your hearts broken before."

Gage frowned. "We've both had people walk out on us. Don't pretend for a second like you're any more wounded than anyone else."

"Sorry," Nik muttered sheepishly. "It's just, I don't know what to do. My whole life as a werewolf, I've dreaded this day. Avoided it, even. After Verika… I was prepared to walk away from the Mark and spend my days alone. Never falling in love again sounded like a dream."

"But…?"

Nik stopped, running a hand over his face as he thought. "I didn't expect to find someone like her. I can't possibly be that lucky."

Gage sighed. "You know what I think? I think you're just looking for excuses to screw things up. That way you don't have to get close to her and you don't risk getting hurt."

Nik scowled at the floor. "Maybe."

Gage was silent a moment. "I think this Mark is the best thing that could have happened to you." When Nik laughed, he said, "No, listen. I'm serious. You look more alive when you're around her. You've always had this shield of bravado up. I knew it was just a mask. You never talked about how Verika leaving you had hurt you, but I could see the pain in your eyes, see the weight of your sorrow in your posture. Now, it's like the real you is shining through. I can see my brother again."

Nik stared at Gage, unsure what to say.

Gage stood and grasped his brother's shoulders, smiling wryly. "Falling in love doesn't make you weak. If anything, when you find the right person for you, it makes you stronger. You support each other. That's how it's supposed to work."

"She'll get tired of my bullshit," Nik said, fear creeping into his heart all over again. Briefly, an image—a nightmare—flickered through his mind. It involved him watching Alara walk away from him forever, saying it would never work. The thought of never seeing her again made him feel like the sun would never rise again.

Gage smirked. "Maybe. But something tells me she's not the type of girl to back down from a fight. If she's your Marked, she's probably a little stubborn and hard-headed."

"Thanks," Nik said dryly.

"Nik, in all seriousness, you shouldn't be scared to let her in. She probably needs you as much as you need her."

Nik thought about what she'd shared with him. It made his blood boil how her family treated her. "Perhaps. I just hope I'm good enough for her."

Gage smiled. "You're one of the best men I know."

Nik slowly smiled back as he let that sink in. "Thanks, man." His brows furrowed. "Did you find out anything about the witch mafia before things went to hell?"

Now it was Gage's turn to pace. "Yes, sort of. I've been talking to Shawna. And don't give me that face. Turns out, she's a mutual friend with our contact."

Nik snorted. "How appropriate she runs with Nightshade scum."

"Anyway," Gage said pointedly, "it seems the more I know, the less I know, if that makes any sense."

"Not at all."

"Well, humor me. Shawna says our contact has connections with some of the Indigo Watchmen."

Nik's brows raised. The Watchmen were the elite task force of the DPI, kind of like private investigators. Only the really serious cases went to them. And if they were involved....

"Apparently, according to what the contact has told her, the Indigo Watchmen have been investigating some fifty-plus killings in the past three months, all in different areas of the country."

"Fifty? Jesus, how come we haven't heard about it? Something like that should be all over the Underworld news."

"That's just it—they've been keeping it covered up because they didn't want to cause widespread panic, especially since they don't know what's going on yet. One thing's linked all the crimes. The victims were all branded with that pentagram symbol."

"The same one Onyx had on his neck?"

"One and the same."

"Shit."

"I know."

Nik worried his lip ring. "Do you think the people who tried to kill the high family were involved with the mafia?"

"It's possible. I just don't know what their motive is. Just last month, they tried to kill my mate. Killing yours, however—a future High Queen—is quite a bit different from taking out a lesser-ranking queen."

"Damn. I wish I knew what kind of game they were playing."

"Don't we all," Gage murmured darkly. "At any rate, we should be extra cautious. Speaking of, where's Alara?"

"Oh, don't worry. She was out in the dining room a moment ago talking to Danica."

Gage frowned. "I hate to say it, but we should probably keep them locked up. Until something's done about the mafia, they could both still be in danger, deserted hotel or not."

"Right." Nik started for the door, then paused. "Where's Jason?"

Gage looked amused. "You mean you can't hear him and Shawna? And I thought I was deaf."

"Ugh." Nik shivered. "Don't remind me of my sexcapades with that psychopath. I hope Jason is into masochism."

"You were, too, if I recall correctly. Maybe you should have been a porn star."

Nik snorted. "Very funny." He shrugged. "I like to experiment. Keeps things interesting. You should try it sometime. I bet Danica would look marvelous in a little leather."

Gage's eyes glowed gold. "I hope you're not imagining my mate naked."

Nik grinned. "Danny? She's like my little sister. Wouldn't dream of it." With that he walked off, but not before he heard Gage mutter, "*Danny*?"

CHAPTER TWELVE

ALARA HAD JUST SLIPPED HER KEYCARD IN THEIR ROOM door when Nik said, "Alara."

She turned, finding him walking toward her. She frowned at the serious look on his face. She'd seen it when the shooting happened. She dubbed it his "warrior face."

"What is it? Did something happen?"

He smiled at her. "Not yet. I'm glad you're going back to the room. I was about to come and get you and take you here anyway."

She raised a brow in question.

He held open the door. "I'll explain inside."

Weird.

She didn't question him. They both walked inside. "What's going on?" she asked, crossing her arms. "Nik, you're scaring me."

He smiled and grasped her arms, running his hands along them. The soothing motion helped calm her nerves a little, though her heart still galloped like a racehorse. "I was just talking to Gage. Since the shooting, we figured we ought to keep both you and Danica hidden—as a precaution."

It took her a moment to figure out why they'd want to hide Danica. "She's the werewolf queen who was attacked last month, right? By that Nightshade wolf?"

Nik's eyes flashed gold for a split second. "Yes. That was Danica." He let go of her arms and went to sit on the bed. She sat down beside him.

"I heard about it," she said carefully, "but I didn't know all the details. What happened?"

Nik searched her eyes as if debating on whether to tell her the truth.

She squeezed his hands. "Whatever it is, I can handle it. Trust me. I'm a lot tougher than I look."

"Oh, I don't doubt it. You'd have to be tough to survive in that world of cutthroat politics." He kissed her forehead and rested his head on her shoulder. It was such a sweet gesture, she took him into her arms, resting her head against his.

"Do you know about the witch mafia?" he asked.

She racked her brain. "Very little. You hear stories, of course. They're almost like an urban legend."

"We suspect they may be involved with hiring the hit on Danica, but we don't have any leads that directly point to them. No one knows their customs, who's a member. Gage and I don't know many witches and warlocks. I have a witch friend in the DPI, and she's keeping her ear to the ground, but so far nothing concrete has come up about the mafia."

Alara frowned. "What makes you think it's even them? Sounds more likely it was a scorned were."

"You would think," he murmured darkly. He explained to her about Onyx and the pentagram symbol on him and told her all about the battle that resulted in his death. By the time Nik was finished, she was wide-eyed. "Holy crap. I had no idea there were wolves buying Black Magic spells."

Nik grinned. "It doesn't surprise me. A nice girl like you probably has no reason to stick her nose in the Underworld's Black Market of forbidden goodies."

She stood, mind racing. "I have to tell my father."

"Whoa, wait up," Nik said, grabbing her arms. "We can't contact your dad."

"Why not? Nik, this is huge! If things like this are happening, he has a right to know so we can put a stop to them!"

Nik looked away. She ducked her head. "What is it? What's the matter?"

It took him a moment to answer. "We can't tell your dad."

"Why not?"

He sighed, running a hand through his hair. "I haven't told Gage this, but I think in the back of his mind he's been wondering the same thing too."

"Which is…?"

He took a deep breath and forced himself to meet her eyes. "I think the reason this kind of activity has been allowed to happen in the first place is because the authorities are turning a blind eye."

She stood there, silent, letting what he'd said sink in. "Wait a minute, are you suggesting my father *knows* about this?"

"It's possible."

A sliver of fear crept into her chest, but she firmly pushed it down and shook her head. "No way. My father's strict and a bit scary sometimes, but he's an honorable man. He would have snuffed out this operation soon as he got word of it."

"Are you sure?"

She swallowed. "Of course I'm sure."

"You hesitated."

She rolled her eyes, growing irritated. "It's insane, Nik! To suggest my father is aiding in criminal activity is treason!"

"But what if I'm right? Huh? What if he's been bought, or worse, what if he's funding it?"

Her jaw dropped in outrage. "How dare you!"

"Look, princess, I know you're daddy's little girl and you hold him on a pedestal. But you have to consider all the possibilities."

"My father's not a criminal," she said firmly, clenching her fists at her sides. "You'll see. He's going to be just as shocked as I was." She started toward the door, but Nik grabbed her arm.

"Where do you think you're going?" he asked, sounding amused.

"To call my father. I can't stay locked away when we have valuable information like this." She tried to take another step, but Nik's grasp held firm.

"You're not going anywhere."

"Ugh!" She jerked her arm free. "Don't tell me what I can and cannot do! I am a princess!"

"Yeah, you're sure acting like one right now," he said, crossing his arms.

"What's that supposed to mean?"

"It means you, like most royals, want to think your shit doesn't stink. But let me tell you something—power corrupts. I've seen it firsthand. How do you think Malachite became so nasty? He wasn't always that way. Some of the wolves I've spoken with who were there at the beginning of his reign told me he wasn't such a bad guy at first. Then he let his power go to his head. There's a good chance your father's been compromised. Until we know all the facts, we can't take any chances."

She crossed her arms. "So, you're what, going to hold me prisoner?"

"Something like that. Don't make me tie you down," he said in a husky voice.

Heat stirred below her navel. She shook her head to clear her thoughts, which only made him grin. She was usually so careful at hiding her emotions. When had he torn through her emotional walls? "I don't think you realize the severity of the situation."

"I understand it damn well."

"Then let me tell my father."

"You're not going back to him."

"Why not?"

"Because I don't want to lose you!"

She blinked, stunned by his outburst.

His shoulders slumped as he stared at her, begging her to stay with his eyes. "I'd given up on love. I've been dreading the mating Fever ever since I first heard about it. I thought after all I'd been through, my heart was broken beyond repair. Then I met you." He stepped closer. "You're my miracle. My angel. My princess. And I don't want to risk the most precious person in the world to me right now. I'm not ready to let you go yet. I doubt I ever will be."

Alara stared at him, speechless. Her heart swelled. "Oh, Nik," she said, eyes dropping to his mouth.

He kissed her before she could get in another breath. She eagerly kissed him back, wrapping her arms around his neck and pulling him closer. She had just started to reach for his shirt when he abruptly broke the kiss. Cold fear flashed in his eyes.

"What is it?" she whispered, almost too afraid to ask.

He swallowed hard. "That was Gage, in my head just now." His eyes met her. "They're here."

"Who?"

"The royal guard. They've found us."

CHAPTER THIRTEEN

T HE HACKLES ON NIK'S INNER WOLF RAISED, PREPPING for battle. If Alara weren't involved, he might have been excited about a fight. Unlike Gage, he didn't have many hold-ups about fighting—when it was needed, of course.

He could smell the fear rising off Alara. Instinctively, he pulled her closer, ears pricked for their enemies' whereabouts.

"How many?" Alara said, glancing around anxiously.

"Don't know."

Nik heard several sets of footsteps approaching down the hall. The rooms were being searched. "Official business of the king," he heard that prick Gerard demand. Fabulous. So he was here too. Nik hid a smirk. At least maybe now he'd get a chance to punch that prick in the face.

"Come on," he said quietly, guiding Alara toward the wall. He grabbed her face, cupping it in his hands so her eyes had to remain on his. "Listen. We can't run. If we go outside, they might shoot us. Same if we both run into the hallway."

She froze, her eyes narrowing as she processed what he'd just said. Her eyes widened. "Don't you dare—"

"It's the only way."

"Sacrificing yourself so I can escape is in no way noble! It's reckless!"

"Alara," he said carefully, holding her gaze. "I need to know you're safe. I'll be fine. They won't lay a hand on me. I'm just going to distract them a bit so you can escape, then I'll be right behind you." He grinned. "I'm a bit of a wild dog when it comes to fights. They won't know what hit 'em."

Alara still didn't look like she believed him, but her shoulders relaxed marginally.

He pressed a swift kiss to her forehead. "When I open the door, you change and run. You'll be faster as a wolf. Don't hesitate no matter what, okay?"

"But—"

"That's my girl." He kissed her hard, allowing himself a brief moment to memorize how she looked in case this didn't end well. He was strong—and she was absolutely right about the reckless part—but he knew he wasn't invincible. There was a real chance he might not come out of this alive. But the thought of having her captured and taken back to a life she didn't want was not an option. If he couldn't be her mate, then he could at least give her her freedom.

He went to the door and grabbed the handle, listening.

They were stopped at the room next door.

Gage.

He had to help his brother and sister-in-law. Inwardly, he swore. Why the hell did this have to happen now?

Because things were looking up for you and Alara, a snide inner voice said. *Should have known things would go to shit.*

Nik's attention snapped back to the hallway as Gerard spoke.

"Check the next room," he commanded. "Kick down the door if you have to."

Nik tensed. "Get ready."

Alara, glaring at him, took up a position behind him. "You better come back to me."

He smiled. "Oh, I plan on it," he said huskily. "And when I do, I plan on doing all kinds of things to you."

A whiff of lust caught his nose. "What kinds of things?"

His sex began to lengthen. "Ssh. You'll distract me. Asskicking's a hard enough calling as it is without a foxy she-wolf to tempt me."

"You're saying you can't handle both?"

He glanced at her. "You wanna bet?"

They were at the door. This was it.

Nik's adrenaline rushed as a wicked smile spread across his lips. *Game on.*

Raising his leg, he kicked the door so hard it flew off the hinges. It barreled into the startled guards, knocking them backwards and onto the floor. "Run!" he yelled.

Alara quickly shifted, becoming an elegant umber-colored wolf, and bolted past him out into the hallway.

"That's her!" Gerard screeched. "Catch her! Alara, come back!"

Nik headed off the two other guards who'd started to chase her, blocking their path. His fists clenched and unclenched at his sides. "You'll have to go through me first. And let me warn you—I won't go down easy."

They lunged, which was their first mistake. They might have been formally trained, but they were pussies. Their punches and kicks were precise, but therein lied their faults. They were predictable. Nik swiftly disarmed them, rendering them both unconscious within thirty seconds. Gerard stared at him, his face turning red with fury.

"GET HIM!"

Nik smiled as more guards rushed around their leader. It was like child's play. Nik laughed as he pummeled his fist into the jaw of one man, knocking him into another. He ducked and punched and kicked and bit until a pile of bodies lay around him.

He chuckled as Gerard gaped at him. "Are these the king's best?" he said, looking around as he cracked his knuckles. "I have to say, I'm a little disappointed. I expected something worthy of protecting royalty. Have these pups even seen combat?"

"You arrogant prick," Gerard hissed.

"What's the matter, love?" Nik said, raising a brow. "Afraid to fight me yourself?"

Gerard's eyes were slits. His eyes blazed gold, and his teeth became fangs. "You should stand down. You have no idea what you're dealing with."

Nik looked around at the bodies of all the men he'd

just beat up. "Actually, I have a pretty good idea. I'm dealing with a bunch of amateurs."

Gerard started forward, rolling up his sleeves. "I'm going to wipe that smug smile off your face."

Nik stood his ground, yawning. "Come and get it, sweetheart."

Gerard roared and charged him, fighting for all he was worth. Nik had to admit he was a little impressed. Gerard was no pushover. His movements were swift, but he could tell he'd learned to fight on the streets.

Which made him dangerous because he wasn't as predictable as the others.

Gerard managed to clip him across the cheek. Nik's face throbbed from the force of the blow. He reached up, smearing blood between his fingertips. "Not bad," he said. "You're fast." He grinned. "I'm faster."

This time, he didn't hold anything back. Gerard started to tire, his movements slowing. He was too pampered. While his fighting skills may be up to par, his stamina was not. "What's wrong?" Nik said, trying hard to control his breathing and still concentrate. He slammed his fist into Gerard's stomach, knocking the wind from him. "Your gym membership expire last year?"

"Shut. Up." Gerard swung, but Nik blocked him, following up with an uppercut that sent the insolent were sprawling backwards across the floor.

He sat up, shaking his head. No doubt the hall was spinning. To his credit, he rose to his feet. He swayed a little, blood dripping down his face from the blow Nik had delivered to his temple. "You think I'm some pampered lapdog, but at least I'm in the king's good graces. Someone like you, with no pedigree to his name, could never hope to win his favor. It doesn't matter you've marked his daughter—the king will never call you son."

"I'm twenty-eight. I haven't needed a daddy since I was thirteen."

"You're not worthy of her."

"Says who? You? Who are you to judge my self-worth? I've had people talking down to me my whole life. My brothers and I grew up in the projects. The town looked down on us as white trash. Were society shuns our pack because of our past maniacal Alpha. You shun all of us because we're not royal. But you know what? Neither are you. I know a street urchin when I see one. You don't learn to fight like that in a castle, pretty boy."

Gerard regarded him for a moment, then smiled slowly. "We are what we pretend to be. And for all your bravado, you're not going to win this fight." His eyes turned steely. "Alara is mine."

Out of nowhere, guards poured down the halls on either side. Nik braced himself. Gerard watched him with a small smile on his face. "Kill him," he said.

They charged.

There were too many; Nik knew that the second he sensed more than ten were signatures. He was good but not that good. Not even he could hold off an army.

Don't be a pussy. You're sure as hell gonna try. Remember who you're fighting for.

Alara's beautiful face flashed through his mind, of her resting her head against his chest and trailing a fingernail down his skin. The memory was enough to drive him into action.

He raced toward them when Gage's door flew open, and he launched himself at the nearest guard. The guy didn't stand a chance. Gage had grown into a kickass fighter. He better have—Nik spent enough time beating his ass when he was training him to take down Malachite. And if he could win in a match with that asshole, these guys were cake.

Together, they fought side by side, taking them on as they came. They disarmed them quickly. Without their guns, they were virtually harmless.

"Shoot them!" Gerard bellowed in outrage.

"We can't, sir!" a guard said. "We'll hit our own men!"

"I don't care! Just take them down!"

The guards looked at each other, giving their leader dirty looks. "The king said not to kill them."

Behind them, Jason and Shawna had joined the brawl.

What took you guys so long? Nik asked them irritably.

Hey, you sounded like you had it covered, Jason said with a smile.

Danica, was all Gage said.

Nik understood. They may be brothers, but since Gage had mated to Danica, her safety came first. He didn't fault him for it. He would've done the same thing if their roles had been reversed. *You should have stayed with her. Where is she?*

In the room, hiding as I told her to. And I couldn't stay hidden any longer. I knew you were outnumbered. I had to act.

Nik smiled at him. *Thanks.*

More werewolves came at them, driving the pack of four together. Nik realized too late what was going on. Gerard's men were boxing them in. Gerard must have issued the command silently, regrouping them. It had crossed Nik's mind this might happen. He had planned on trying to get them outside, but the opportunity had never presented itself. Before he knew it, the guards had them surrounded, their weapons raised to their heads.

Gerard smiled at them. "You've fought valiantly. But it appears I have won."

"We're still standing," Nik said in a steely voice.

"Not for long. Alara! I know you can hear me."

Nik silently prayed his mate had run away as he'd asked her to. When he picked up her signature nearby, drawing closer, he swore. *No! Stay back! It's a trap!*

"Alara," Gerard bellowed, "either come out now and surrender, or I kill your friends."

"No!" Nik shouted, but it was too late.

Alara's voice rang through the hall. She stood naked at the other end, chin lifted defiantly, eyes glued to Gerard. "Here I am. Let them go."

Gerard pushed forward through the crowd, removing his jacket and using it to cover Alara. Nik growled, but Gage grabbed his arm to keep him from rushing off to pummel Gerard some more. He should have knocked him out when he had the chance. If this mess was anyone's fault it was his. He'd had his opportunity and he'd blown it.

He cursed.

Gerard gazed at Alara with concern, reaching for her

face. "Are you hurt?"

She turned her head away from his touch. "No," she said coldly, glaring at him.

His hand clenched and fell back at his side. "I can see we'll have a lot to talk about," he said tersely, taking her shoulders. "You're coming with me." He looked back at his guards.

Nik knew he was issuing another silent command, and his heart started pounding.

Alara turned around, fighting to break free of Gerard's grasp. "Wait! Stop!" She dug her heels in. Two more guards stepped forward and took her.

"Handle her with care," Gerard instructed as if giving them instructions about handling a package.

"No!" She fought against her captors. Her eyes caught Nik's before she vanished around the corner. "Nik!" she screamed.

"Alara!" he yelled. He broke free of Gage's grasp.

"Wait, Nik!" Gage yelled, but Nik was already driving his fists into people's faces and stomachs—whatever he saw first.

The guards closed in on him. It took five of them to take him down, but at last, his knees bit into the carpet as he was forced down. Behind him, his friends had been taken captive as well.

Gerard stalked toward him and jerked his face up to meet his eyes. He smiled. "Looks like I win." He leaned forward, his voice lowered so only Nik would hear.

"I can't wait to fuck your mate."

Nik growled viciously, snapping his teeth. He wanted

to rip Gerard's throat out. Gerard backed out of the way just in time. Composing himself, he gave a lazy snap of his fingers.

Someone raised the butt of their gun from the corner of Nik's vision. As he turned his head, something hard collided against his skull. Pain blossomed through his brain, blurring his vision.

He slumped forward as someone began tying his arms and legs together. The heavy darkness around his vision grew thicker until he could no longer hold his eyes open.

"Ala... ra," he rasped with his last breath before he couldn't think anymore.

CHAPTER FOURTEEN

ALARA KEPT SCREAMING NIK'S NAME ALL THE WAY TO the car.

"Forgive me, Your Highness," one of the guards said, right before placing a gag in her mouth. They forced her upside the car, tying her hands and feet together, then they lifted her into the backseat.

She kicked and struggled, but all she succeeded in doing was rubbing her wrists and ankles raw against her binds. Her pulse pounded in her head as the worst played through her mind. What if Nik was already dead? Gage? Danica? The thought of them lying in a pool of their own blood made her sick.

A tear rolled down her cheek, but she refused to cry. She wasn't going to seem weak to Gerard, whom she hated more than anyone else in the world right now.

She heard him outside the car. "Where is she?" A moment later, he opened the door. The first thing she did was try to kick him.

He caught her feet, his eyes immediately going to her binds. His face went red. "What the hell is this?" he roared, rounding on the guards who'd tied her up and tossed her in the car.

"Um, she was resisting," one said, fidgeting.

"She is our crown princess! Untie her at once!"

"Ye—yes, sir!"

They gently helped her out of the car and undid her binds. She tore the gag out herself soon as her hands were free, and threw it to the ground. Gerard stared at the raw blisters circling her wrists and ankles. With a growl, he turned and pummeled his fist into the face of the closest guard. He then stalked to the other and did the same. Blood spewed from both their noses, which were now set crookedly.

"How *dare* you harm her," he seethed. "Let me make this clear: You both report straight to the dungeons when we get back. You will each receive twenty lashes."

Their faces went pale.

Alara had had about enough. Livid, she tapped Gerard on the shoulder. Soon as he turned to look at her, she let her hand fly across his face. His head jerked to the side, and he blinked, stunned.

"They will receive no such punishment," she said in her strongest voice. "They were only doing what they thought best." She jerked her arms up. "They're only blisters. They'll heal."

Gerard recovered, straightening his shirt. "Lady Alara—"

"That's an order," she said coldly. "Or shall I tell my father you're questioning my command now?"

His jaw ticked. The guards looked anxiously between them. At last, Gerard nodded curtly. "Very well. As you wish." He opened the front passenger-side door and motioned toward the car. "After you, my lady."

She glanced around. The parking lot was full. He must have brought half his guards to go after her. There was no way she could escape. They might be loyal to the crown, but they were still his soldiers.

She looked at the car. "Where's Nik?"

"Unharmed, so long as you cooperate."

Conniving bastard. She chastised herself for ever being attracted to him. Why couldn't she see how brutal he was before?

Because you were seeing only what you wanted to see— your prince charming. You're no better than Izzy's brainless friends. You saw a pretty face and overlooked the heart of stone within.

Glaring at him, she reluctantly got in the car. Gerard shut the door, muttered something to his guards, then walked around the other side and climbed in the driver's seat. "Buckle up," he said quietly as he started the engine.

She threw daggers at him with her gaze, not moving.

He looked at her pointedly. "Please?"

Think of Nik. She gritted her teeth and buckled her seat belt.

He took off, several cars falling in behind them on the open road.

They drove in tense silence for several minutes.

"You're welcome," he finally said.

"I don't recall saying 'thank you.'"

His grip tightened on the steering wheel. "I rescued you."

"You coerced me," she snapped. "There's a difference."

"Oh, come on, Your Highness," he said, rolling his eyes. "He kidnapped you."

"I left of my own free will!"

Gerard's brows furrowed as he spared her a glance. He pressed his lips together until the blood drained out of them. "Why?" he finally asked.

She blinked, caught off guard. She'd been expecting a reprimand. She found it surprisingly difficult to say the answer. "Because if he was leaving, I couldn't stay."

"You can't tell me you love him."

"No," she admitted. "But I think I could. And that chance is worth holding on to."

He stared straight ahead, then chuckled sadly. "The first time I saw you, I thought you were the most beautiful woman I'd ever laid eyes on. Your passion for life shone through in everything you did. You weren't like the rest of them. You made life at the palace bearable. You didn't treat me as street scum, as the thief the king decided to adopt and make into a soldier instead of executing him. You saw value in a human being other royals had deemed as worthless."

"You're not worthless," she said, her anger leaving her.

He turned off the road, heading down a dirt path. "You wouldn't say that if you knew what I was capable of."

She frowned, looking around as the drive grew

bumpier. She sat up straighter. "This isn't the way to the castle."

"It's a shortcut."

He's lying, a warning voice whispered inside her head.

Swallowing hard and trying to get a grip on her fears before they took control of her, she said, "None of us can help who we've been. It's what we do now that counts."

His mouth twitched in the imitation of a smile. "I wish it were as easy as that."

"It can be. It's all about the choices you make, right here, right now."

He froze. Her heart pounded in her chest as she watched his reaction.

He's up to something. Don't trust him.

This time, she decided to listen to her gut. She discreetly reached for the door handle.

His hand shot up, locking it at the last second. She pulled, but it wouldn't budge. "What's going on?"

For a moment, she thought he hadn't heard her. He continued to stare straight ahead, face blank. Then his gaze finally met hers.

"I'm sorry, Alara." Regret shone in his eyes. "Please understand I didn't have a choice."

The blood drained from her face as an eerie chill crept over her. "What's going on?" she whispered. "Gerard, what have you done?"

His eyes dropped to her arm just as something pricked her. She lowered her gaze, catching him withdrawing a syringe.

Her heart started pounding. "What did you give...

me?" The wave of dizziness hit her with surprising quickness. In the blink of an eye, her thoughts began to slow to a crawl, and her vision blurred as she slumped in the seat.

The last thing she felt was Gerard's cold fingers brushing the hair out of her eyes.

CHAPTER FIFTEEN

WHEN NIK CAME TO, THE FIRST THING HE NOTICED WAS he had a bitching headache.

"Christ," he groaned. It felt like with the slightest movement his brain would drip right out of his ears. He sniffed.

Was that… gasoline? God, it was strong, like he'd been doused in it.

As his addled brain slowly came to, he took note of his still blurry surroundings. It was dark. He and Gage were tied to the bed, back in one of the rooms. They seemed to be the only captives. Where the hell were Danica, Jason, and Shawna?

Something wet splashed him in the face. He nearly gagged when he went to lick his lips. "What the hell?"

"Shit. This one's awake." Two of Gerard's lackeys stood over him. "Should we knock him out?"

"Nah. Let him roast. People burn the same whether

120

they're awake or unconscious."

Nik's eyes snapped open, his senses fully wired. He looked around. Dark stains ran across the carpet as if the whole room had been doused in—

"Oh, my God." He immediately began working at his binds, but it was no use. Someone knew what they were doing when it came to tying knots because the rope wasn't budging. "You assholes think this is justice?" he roared as they walked toward the door. "Think about Alara. She's a royal, a high were. If you kill me, she won't be able to complete the mating ceremony. She'll lose her ranking—"

"Good thing we're not loyal to the crown." One of the guys grinned. "The hell if I care what happens to some spoiled princess. Pretty soon, it won't matter whether she's mated or not."

They slammed the door and locked it. A trail of gasoline went under the door.

Nik's heart slammed against his ribcage. What the hell did they mean "it wouldn't matter soon?" Were they going to do something to Alara?

He had to get out of here.

Frantically, he worked at breaking free, nearly tearing his limbs off in the process. "Gage!" he yelled. "Dammit, wake up!"

When Gage wouldn't move, he racked his brain. Left with no other choice, he focused on shifting his teeth to fangs. "Sorry, bro," he said, right before chomping down on his brother's shoulder.

That got his attention.

Gage's eyes snapped open with a gasp. He looked

down, incredulous. "You bit me."

"Had to. You were in a coma. Heads-up. We're about to be burned alive. Are your binds loose at all?"

Gage blinked several times as if trying to clear his head. His gaze turned serious and he started shuffling around. "It's no use," he said between gritted teeth. "Someone knows what they're doing."

"We had to get intelligent henchmen. Typical."

"And not just that," Gage said, his gaze drunken. "They've injected us with something. We should be able to break through rope. I feel like that time I came down with mono and had to be put in the hospital."

Nik frowned. He'd noticed the absence of strength too, but he thought maybe he'd imagined it because he had a concussion.

A match struck from outside the door. Nik and Gage both held their breaths, right before flames started crawling along the floor, right toward them. The fire crept closer and closer, seeming to gain speed as it drew near.

Nik and Gage both struggled more violently, but they might as well have wrestled steel. They clearly weren't going anywhere, and any minute now, they would both be werewolf-kabobs.

The door shuddered as someone tried forcing it open. A moment later, they succeeded, and Danica rushed into the room carting a fire extinguisher. She wasted no time. Foam shot through the air, ending the fire's life an inch or two from their feet. White dust settled around the room, coating the furniture in a powdery sheen.

Danica rushed forward and immediately started

working at their binds with a switchblade. Within a minute, Gage was free. He hugged Danica fiercely. "I thought I'd lost you," he said hoarsely into her hair.

She clung to him, breathing hard. "I stayed hidden back in our room and waited for them to leave. When I saw them light that match... God, Gage."

"Sssh," he said soothingly, stroking her hair. "It's fine, love. We're safe."

Nik cleared his throat. They both looked at him as if suddenly remembering he was there. "Not that I want to get in the way of true love or nothing, but I would appreciate being cut free."

Danica smiled and wiped away a stray tear that had fallen down her cheek. She blushed as she leaned in to work at his binds. "Of course. Sorry."

"Nothing to apologize for. You saved our lives."

Once he was free, he flexed his wrists. "Much better." His eyes looked at Danica. "Since when do you carry around a knife?"

She got a proud look on her face as she lifted her chin. "I used to live in the ghetto. Old habits die hard I guess."

Nik raised a brow. "Because Moonstruck is full of gangsters and thugs."

"It's not the gangsters and thugs I'm worried about—it's the werewolves."

Nik blinked, amused. "Right." They all stood, and Nik became all business. "Do you know which way they went?"

"Out the front. All the others are gone. Guess these guys are so far down the totem pole they got left behind to do the dirty work."

"Did you see Jason and Shawna?" Gage asked.

She nodded. "They shot them up with something, then tied them up and blindfolded them before loading them up into the cars and driving off."

Gage swore and ran a hand over his face. It was every Alpha's worst nightmare—not being there to take care of his packmates, the people who counted on him to protect them.

Nik silently prayed they were all right. He started forward. "We can't let those two wannabe murderers escape. They may be our only lead to finding Alara and the others."

He ran out the door—or stumbled was more like it. His balance was thrown way off. He had to keep a hand pressed against the wall to keep from falling over. Same went for Gage, though he had Danica to lean on.

They stopped to pick up some abandoned guns off the bodies that had been left behind. Nik and Gage checked the cartridges. "Still loaded. Good."

They crept toward the front entrance. Nik's heart raced faster with every step. His mind kept reeling back to the moment Verika had left him and the crushing sensation that had followed soon after. It was happening again. He was losing someone he cared about.

They paused by the doors and peeked out. The guards were having a freaking smoke break.

"You have got to be joking," Nik muttered.

"Shall we sneak up on them?" Gage said.

Nik nodded. "We'll rush them."

Danica rolled her eyes. "You're such men. All brute force and no strategy." She ripped the seam of her shirt so her cleavage was fully exposed. "Allow me."

Gage's eyes grew big. "Danica, no!" he said, swiping for her, but she'd already waltzed out the door.

She walked right past the men, letting her hair down and ruffling it. "Hey, boys," she said with a wide smile. "Are you lonely tonight?"

They looked at each other and chuckled. "Maybe. We don't get to enjoy the company of she-wolves very often in our line of work."

"Is that so?" she said as Nik and Gage crept out the doors and behind the men. "Well, I was going to offer a threesome, but if you're too busy...." She started to walk away, and one of the men grabbed her.

"Hold up there, sweetheart. We didn't say nothin' about being too busy."

She smiled coldly. "Good. I was hoping you'd stick around a bit longer."

At once, Nik and Gage pressed the barrels of their guns to the backs of the guys' heads. "Drop your weapons," Gage demanded in a stone-cold voice. "Now."

They both froze, moving only to do as they were told. "How the hell did you two escape?"

Danica twiddled her fingers, then formed a fist and decked both of them, one right after the other. "That was for trying to kill my mate and my brother-in-law. Sort of."

She and Gage weren't technically married yet. Mating was enough in were law to practically make them married, but Danica still clung to her human traditions. She wanted a wedding, though no date had been set yet.

Gage and Nik's brows shot up at the same time. Nik

whistled as the men swore, clutching at their jaws. "Nice one, sis. We might make a fighter out of you yet."

She grinned at him.

Nik grabbed one of the men and put the gun against his temple. "Now, where were we? Oh, yes. We were at the part where you tell us where to find our friends."

CHAPTER SIXTEEN

ALARA CAME TO WITH A GROAN. THE LIGHTS WERE TOO bright. She hadn't had a migraine like this since she was a child.

She was lying on something soft, like a bed. Candles were lit about the room, but her vision was still too blurry for her to make out much. When she finally did see clearly, she wished she was still unconscious.

What at first she thought was a bed was actually an altar. The candles were lined up in a star shape, of which she was in the center—a pentagram.

Her heart started racing as she tried to sit up and found her wrists and ankles had been bound to the altar. She struggled, but it was useless. Why was she so weak? It was like she'd had all her strength zapped out of her. She craned her head enough to see what she was wearing. Someone had removed Gerard's coat and dressed her in a red silk nightgown.

"Ah, you're awake," said a dark voice that sent chills up her spine.

No. No, it can't be....

She slowly lifted her eyes to see her father standing outside the pentagram. Gerard stood behind him, his face conflicted. He wouldn't meet her eyes. Both men wore long, black cloaks with a pentagram symbol etched in silver thread and a word in a language she couldn't read in the middle.

Her blood ran cold. "What's going on?" she asked, the words coming out choked. She could barely breathe, her heart was beating so fast.

Her father's black gaze regarded her with disgust. "I'm fulfilling my rights to the Order of the Sun."

"What Order? What are you talking about?" She thought of what Nik told her, and she looked again at the symbol on their robes. "You're part of the witch mafia."

He snorted. "People have started calling it that, but yes, they're one and the same."

"But you're not a warlock."

His eyes flashed gold, then green. "Not a whole one, anyway." He raised both hands and the ground began to shake. A moment later, he dropped his hands and the earthquake stopped.

Her eyes widened. "You're a Green Warlock?"

"My mother was a Green Witch. As was her mother before her, and so on. Her gift for earth magic passed on to me."

"But…" Her face scrunched in confusion. "You don't have the signature of a warlock."

"Are you daft, girl?" he said sharply. "Signatures can be masked, if you know the right people. Do you think our family got this high up without some magical help?"

"I thought…" she stammered, blinking back tears. "I thought it was because the people admired you. They respected our bloodline."

Alara had always suspected her father had obtained his power through other means. She just wanted to believe he was better than that, that he wasn't corrupt. Nik was right all along. He had been right about everything. Her father hadn't just been turning an eye to the witch mafia activities because he'd been paid off—he'd helped them because he was actually in the Order.

She felt sick.

"Don't worry," he said soothingly. His attempt at making her feel better only made her skin crawl. "Gerard injected you with a sedative. It started to wear off, which is why you woke up, but you'll still feel the side effects long enough for us to complete the ritual."

She could barely swallow. "What ritual?"

He grinned, stepping into the circle. He looked like a demon. "Our Mistress has great plans," he purred, lifting a dagger from the inside of his cloak. "Three werewolves of royal descent must be sacrificed in order for the spell to work."

She couldn't take her eyes off the dagger. Her mind raced, reviewing what he'd said. "Three…" Her eyes snapped to his. "Where are Mother and Izzy?"

He grinned. "Your mother is dead," he said without remorse. "I'd been waiting years to drive a blade through that cheating whore's heart."

A single tear ran down Alara's cheek as she shook with anger. She didn't know how to feel. Her mother was dead. She'd always resented her mother in a way, but now she just felt… empty. The familiar numbness was taking over, her emotional self-defense mechanism. God, it hurt so much to feel.

"What are you talking about?" she rasped. "Mother was loyal to you."

Her father laughed outright. "You naive, stupid girl. How the hell do you think you came about? Why do you think you look so different from the rest of us purebloods? Your mother loved a commoner, her old flame before she was married off to me via an arranged marriage after we marked. But it was too late. He'd already planted his filthy seed inside her belly."

Alara tried to process this as her father kept talking.

"Oh, she tried to pass it off as mine, of course," he said. "But I had a paternity test completed when you were a baby and started showing unusual physical characteristics. Imagine my disappointment and rage when I found out I was not the father of my firstborn child. We had to keep it quiet, of course, to avoid a scandal."

Alara glared at him, her shock turning to anger. "You never loved me. It all makes sense now."

He stared at her, thinking. "No. I don't suppose I ever did," he admitted with indifference.

Her heart all but turned to steel at that point. "I hate you. I swear on Mother's grave, I will end your life if it's the last thing I do."

Her father smiled at her. "Empty threats, my dear. Pretty soon, you won't feel or think much of anything at all." He raised the dagger, the tip angled above her heart. In the background, Gerard began chanting. Shadows swirled through the air, crackling with purple energy.

Black Magic.

"You'll be sacrificing your only heirs if you kill me and Izzy," Alara said.

"Do you think that matters to me? My Mistress has promised me immortality if I succeed in doing this for her. I won't need heirs if I live forever." His gaze darkened, growing more power-hungry. "Do you think any of those other fools knows what it takes to rule? I am the only High King!"

He started to bring the dagger down.

Alara sucked in her last breath, eyes wide with the knowledge she was about to die.

I'm sorry, Nik.

A gunshot rang from across the room, and her father cried out as the dagger flew from his hand. It landed on the floor with a clatter.

Alara looked up and gasped. "Nik."

Nik, Gage, and Danica stood at the other end of the room. Gage and Nik both had guns. "Get the hell away from my mate," Nik said, stepping forward.

Her father chuckled darkly, hands raised as he slowly backed away. "I knew you would come for her. Which was why I took your friends as a little collateral."

"Where are Jason and Shawna?" Gage demanded.

"Safe—for now." He didn't give them any warning.

Green energy shot out of his hands, straight toward them. Nik and the others ducked out of the way just as the bolts singed the walls.

"Finish the ritual!" the king screamed at Gerard.

He dove for the knife, but Gage was quicker. He shifted and pounced on Gerard, who shifted at the last second. The two great wolves snapped and brawled with one another.

"Danica, get the knife!" Nik yelled.

She ran for it, scooping it up and scrambling to her feet.

"No!" the king yelled. He flicked his wrist. The foundation shook as vines broke through the flooring, climbing up the walls. One whipped about the room, lassoing Danica's ankle. She went down hard, dropping the dagger and sending it skidding across the floor as the vine pulled.

Nik growled and shot again at the king, but the king deflected it with a green energy shield.

One of the wolves yowled nearby in pain; Alara couldn't tell in the blur of fur who was wounded. Blood streaked across the floor. Danica took a switchblade out of her pocket and started carving the vine around her ankle. It let go with a shriek, and she grabbed the gun Gage had dropped when he'd charged Gerard.

She ran to Alara as Nik started unloading his clip on her father, who had to keep his focus on deflecting the bullets. His whole body was nearly encased in a green, shifting bubble of earth magic.

Danica sawed away at the binds until Alara's hands were free. She shifted her nails into claws and cut away at her right ankle's binds while Danica worked on the left. "Thanks," she said once she was free.

Danica helped her off the table. "Don't mention it."

Her knees shook.

Nik's gun clicked, signaling the clip was empty. He looked at the gun, then threw it at the king as hard as he could. The king blinked in surprise, deflecting it, but by the time he looked up, Nik had transformed into a large brown wolf and was charging him.

Her father's energy shield flickered for a second as his mouth dropped open in surprise.

That was all the distraction Nik needed. He collided with the king, knocking him into a wall. The king's eyes glowed gold right before he transformed into the massive charcoal-colored wolf that was the High King. He was definitely bigger than Nik, and just as brutally violent. The two clawed and snapped at each other, fangs bared.

Danica and Alara watched them. Alara warred with herself. What should she do? She couldn't erase the image of her father from her mind. Then she remembered he hadn't been there for a single birthday, had never told her he was proud of her. All those smiles, all those acknowledgements of her existence… they had only ever been while they were in the company of others. Alone, he acted like she wasn't even there at all.

Her hands shook, slowly becoming fists.

He's evil, Alara, she told herself. *You should help your mate before it's too late.*

Across the room, Gage flew into the wall. He shook his head as he got up, but before he did, Gerard had already run out the door. Danica ran to Gage, supporting him as he transformed back into a man. He was covered in bite-marks and lacerations that were slowly healing. "I'm fine," he said through gritted teeth. "Where's Nik?"

"Fighting the king."

"*What*?" His eyes snapped forward. He struggled to his feet. "I have to help him."

"No! Gage, you're in no condition to fight."

"Danica, if I don't help him, he could die!"

Alara's heart skipped a beat. Gage was right. Nik was a terrific fighter, but her father was the larger wolf. She could tell every hit walloped Nik. Many more of those, and he'd be toast.

She did the only thing she could do. Mind made up, she shifted and charged her father from behind. She launched herself onto his back, biting at his neck, trying to get a good grip. Her father howled in fury. He bucked, trying to throw her off, but she held on.

Her father reared, pitching himself against the vine-covered wall. Alara yelped as thorns dug into her back. Her grip faltered, and she started to slide off. Nik seized the opportunity—he opened his jaws and locked them around her father's exposed throat before jerking once. Blood spewed, and her father gurgled out another howl. He fell to the side, paws slipping on the blood-soaked floor as he tried getting up. Slowly, his fur became flesh and he was a man once more. His eyes found Alara.

"Curse... you," he rasped, then stilled, his eyes going vacant.

Alara shifted back with a sob. *Oh, my God. I just killed*

my own father. What have I done? She fell to the floor beside her father, grasping his cold, dead hand. "I'm sorry," she said. "I'm so sorry."

Tears poured down her face, and she shook uncontrollably. Nik came up behind her and wrapped her up in what was left of the shredded nightgown. He held her in his arms as she cried, clinging to him. Her adoration for him was the only thing that made sense in the world, the only thing that was keeping her from falling completely apart.

She had just helped murder her father. What kind of a person did that make her?

Overwhelming guilt weighed her down as Nik rocked her.

"I'm here," he murmured into her hair, pressing a kiss against her sweat-dampened forehead. "I'll always be here."

"Don't leave me," she whispered.

"I don't plan on it. Ever."

CHAPTER SEVENTEEN

It took a few hours to calm Alara down. Nik never left her side. He was surprised she was able to pull herself together in that length of time. She had to be traumatized. The king might have been psychotic as hell, but he was still her father.

They all sat in one of the meeting rooms, being tended to by physicians. Jason and Shawna had been rescued from the dungeons. They had been given the same sedative Gerard had given Alara. It was almost entirely out of their systems now, a process that had been sped along by a counter-elixir they'd been treated with.

Gerard was nowhere to be found. Neither was the dagger that had almost taken Nik's mate away from him forever. They'd all assumed he'd snatched it up during his escape.

Guards and DPI agents swarmed about the place, turning it over for evidence of the king's involvement with the witch mafia. Apparently, right before the ritual, the king had enchanted the guards so they were literally asleep on their feet. The spell had broken once the king had died. The guards had no idea what had happened.

All of them were still treating Alara as the acting leader. She'd told Nik what the king had revealed to her about her parentage. Since she was a bastard, she was ineligible for the crown. It fell to the next pureblood in line, which would be Izzy.

If only they could find her.

Alara had insisted on searching for her too, but her legs kept giving out. The aftereffects of the sedative, coupled with her shock, had taken a toll on her body, and she was forced to stay behind, at least for now, and rest.

Nik could tell it made her incredibly anxious, though. It would have driven him nuts too, if Gage were missing and he was unable to search for him himself.

Nik rubbed Alara's shoulders. "Don't worry. They'll find her."

"What if they don't?" she said despondently. She had her elbows propped up on the table and was chewing on her nails. "What if she's already dead?"

He'd considered that possibility, but no way was he going to voice it out loud. Alara needed encouragement, not heartbreak. "She's not. I bet any minute now, we'll hear word she's been found and is alive and well."

Alara grunted, not looking like she much believed him. It was the same reaction she'd had when the DPI told her they'd found the queen's body. She'd stared blankly ahead, not looking like she was really there. He couldn't imagine the shock she'd endured. It was like her brain had shut down, refusing to process anything. He remembered feeling that way when Verika left, after his father died, when his mother left... all the times he'd ever felt alone in the world. The grief would hit later. And he planned on being there to support her when it did.

An agent entered the room. Like the others, she was dressed in a freshly pressed pantsuit. Her hair was worn up in a tight bun that pulled at her face. He hadn't seen any of the agents crack a smile. It was what made Verika stand out among them. She wasn't like the others. She felt more human and less robotic.

"We've subpoenaed the phone calls on the king's private line. We thought you should have a look at this."

To Nik's surprise, she handed the phone records not to Alara but to Gage. He took them, frowning deeper as he read. "This can't be possible." His eyes met Nik's. "Crescent Manor's number is on here."

"What?" Nik reached for the paper, and Gage handed it to him. He quickly scanned it, finding Crescent Manor's number listed more than once. It felt like someone had slapped the breath out of him. "Shit."

"Mr. Johnson," the agent said, addressing Gage, "As you know, we have been unable to find any more leads on the calls you had us subpoena from your manor. Not only were they untraceable until now, they were also encrypted by cloaking magic." She looked proud. "Since we now know where the calls were going to, we've been able to successfully break the spell masking those interactions."

"And?" Gage said quietly. He was perfectly still, as

if bracing himself. Danica rested a hand on his arm and squeezed.

"We've listened to the calls," the agent said, crossing her arms. "Do you know an 'Erik Lacross?'"

"No fucking way," Nik and Gage swore at the same time.

Danica's eyes widened with recognition. "Is that the same Erik…?"

"Yes," Gage said. He ran a hand over his face, which had gone white with shock. "He went with us to the witch's cabin."

"Oh, my God," she breathed, sitting back and covering her mouth with her hands.

Alara looked at Nik, a question in her eyes and a frown on her lips. He shook his head. *I'll explain later*, he told her.

"He talked to the king twice, it looks like," the agent explained. "The king paid him to inform him when you"—she pointed to Gage—"started your mating Fever. He wasn't given any other details as to why the king wanted to know this information."

"So it wasn't the mafia who put out the hit on Danica," murmured Gage. "It was the king. But why?"

"We'll do some more investigating and let you know if we find out anything else." She left, leaving the room in stunned silence.

"Wow," Nik finally said. His mind was blown. Never in a million years would he have thought noble Erik would be capable of being bribed. Then again, he did have a sick little sister a few states away to financially support. A little sister the pack now fully supported since he was gone. It was the least they could do for his service to the pack, traitor or not. They girl didn't do anything wrong.

"I can't believe it," Gage finally said, shaking his head. "I trusted Erik with my life. Now I know he was responsible for setting off the assassination attempt on my mate."

"The question is why?" Nik muttered darkly.

The room stewed on that a bit. First, Danica was almost murdered by the king. Then the bastard ordered hits on his own family. That plan failed, so he attempted to complete the ritual on his own.

What the hell was the Underworld coming to?

The hairs along the backs of his arm pricked like they did when a storm was coming and electricity was in the air. The question was, what exactly did this Mistress Black hope to achieve with all this bloodshed? What was her end game?

There was a lot of movement out in the hall. Voices rose as conversations were thrown about. One piece in particular stood out to Nik.

They were talking about the missing princess, Isabelle.

Alara heard it too. Her head snapped up, and she bolted out of her seat so fast the chair nearly toppled over.

Nik followed after her.

She tore the door open. "What's happened? Have you found Izzy?"

"I told you to keep your voices down," snapped one of the agents. Then she muttered something about "Damn werewolf hearing" before smiling. It looked fake, like she was out of practice. She probably was. "We have located

Princess Isabelle."

"Well, where is she?" Alara interrupted, trying to see around the woman.

The agent's smile faltered. "Ma'am, I need you to calm down."

Oh, shit. Anytime a law enforcement officer said those words, you knew they were prepping you for something bad.

Alara grew more hysterical. "I want to see her. I need to see my baby sister!"

When the guards tried to restrain her, she tore off past them, running down the hall.

The agent spoke into her walkie. "The princess is coming your way. Stop her from getting through at all costs."

"Why?" Nik said. "What's going on?"

The agent turned her nose up at him. "And who are you?"

"I'm her mate, dammit," he growled. "Now tell me what the hell is going on."

The agent blinked in surprise. She opened up her mouth to speak when Alara's scream echoed down the hall.

At first, Alara didn't want to believe what she was seeing.

"Izz…y," she whispered in horror.

Her knees gave out and she started to go down. Two strong arms wrapped around her. The smell of the woods enveloped her—Nik's smell.

She heard him swear as he tried making her look away,

but she refused. They were sitting in a secret room at the end of one of the castle's many hidden passageways. Izzy must have been kept prisoner here. Alara couldn't imagine how alone and scared she must have felt, in the darkness by herself, waiting to die.

Her sister had been laid on an altar similar to the one she herself had been strapped to. Alara couldn't tear her eyes off her sister's bloody body, the dagger still embedded in her chest. Gerard must have found the knife and finished what her father started. Her sister's eyes stared back at her, as if to say, "Why didn't you try to protect me?"

Behind her, on the wall, was a message scrawled in blood.

The ritual is complete. Beware the coming darkness.

The ritual… three royal werewolves. Her mother, father, and now her baby sister.

Alara was an orphan. In one fell swoop, she'd lost her entire family.

The shock slowly wore off, replaced by something darker. Something with more purpose.

Rage.

Seething, she stood on one shaky leg at a time.

Nik hovered near her elbow. "Come away, Alara."

"No," she said firmly, staring down at her sister. "I need to see this. I need to remember who's done this to me so I'll be strong enough to face what's ahead."

"You're not making any sense, love," he murmured.

Feeling cold fury burning through her veins, she turned and looked her mate dead in the eyes.

"I'm going to kill Mistress Black."

CHAPTER EIGHTEEN

THREE DAYS.

That was how long Izzy—and the rest of her family—had been in the ground. Yet, it seemed like a lifetime ago. Last week, she was a princess. Now... now she had no clue who she was. She didn't even know how she was supposed to feel about all this. Her emotions had been all over the place, swinging from grief to anger to elation that she was finally, truly *free*. And under it all rested the simmering anger she'd felt as she'd watched blood run down the arm and fingers of her little sister.

The funeral had been all over the Underworld news. It was the grandest funeral the werewolf community, and probably the whole Underworld, had ever seen. Alara had wanted to keep it a private ceremony because she honestly didn't think she could handle media attention right now, but somehow it seemed like the whole world had showed up for the burials. She should feel flattered, in a way, that people thought so highly of her family.

And it had all been a lie. The Crescent name, the way they had achieved their power. Not through honor, not through their noble actions, but through manipulation and greed. Her family had never been the champions of justice and pillars of righteousness they'd pretended to be. No, she was beginning to doubt there had ever been much honor in her family legacy at all.

Alara stared at herself in the mirror. She was in her room. Flowers people had sent to show their sympathy dripped from every surface. She knew people meant well, but good lord, the smell was about to drive her up the wall.

She'd plucked a single red rose from one of the arrangements to wear in her hair. A bit macabre, perhaps, since it came from a funeral bouquet, but it looked pretty against the white ceremonial mating robe she now wore. Her long hair was still damp on the ends. She'd twisted it and draped it over one shoulder. She wore no make-up—she saw no need. Nik already knew what she looked like at her most vulnerable, and oh, tonight she would be vulnerable.

What if she did something wrong? What if she screwed everything up and the bonding spell didn't work?

The Mark glittered in the moonlight streaming through her open curtains. She couldn't believe it was already the end of the month.

Her Blood Moon was here.

And tonight, she would forever bind herself to the man she was growing to love.

A soft knock came at the door, interrupting her jitters.

She cleared her throat and called, "Come in."

The door opened, and her breath left her as her mate strolled into the room. His broad frame was covered in the robe. She knew the hard muscles that lay beneath, and she licked her lips as a wave of heat rushed below her navel.

"Hello," he said with a small, sexy smile as he came up behind her and wrapped his arms around her torso.

She leaned her head back against his shoulder, closing her eyes and breathing in the scent of his pine body wash. It was such a refreshing change from the flowers that permeated the room. "You smell nice," she murmured absently.

He snorted. "Always a plus." They were silent a moment. She opened her eyes, finding him staring back at her, a slight frown to his lips.

"What is it?" she asked gently. "What's wrong?"

He swallowed and started to look away, then held her gaze. "You don't have to do this."

She sighed. "Nik, we've been through this—"

"Please, hear me out."

She pressed her lips together, waiting. Her heart started to pound. *He's changed his mind about this. He's going to kick you to the curb by letting you down gently*, her fears sang.

He slowly turned her and grasped her hands in his. "Alara, before I met you, I didn't realize how much I'd needed you, to feel close to someone again. But..." He squeezed her hands. At first she thought he meant it as an emphasizing gesture, then she felt a tremble.

His hands were shaking.

He closed his eyes and took a deep breath. "But I know you've been through a lot. What happened to your family was... God, Alara. I can't begin to imagine what you're going through. And I want you to know I'll always be here for you, no matter what."

She braced herself. *Here it comes.*

She could hear his heart. It was beating nearly as fast as her own. The emotion swirling in his eyes made her breathless. He reached up and cupped her cheek, tracing the rough pad of his thumb along her skin. "God, you're so beautiful," he murmured. "Since the moment I met you, I've been unable to stop thinking about you. These past few days have been both dream and nightmare, and despite the hard times, I've felt myself falling harder for you every day. But I know you have a kingdom to rule, and lots of other people will need you. I don't want to get in your way."

Her shoulders sank with relief, and she smiled at him in amusement. "First of all, I'm not a princess. Well, I still sort of am. I'm half royal, apparently. So, technically I'm ineligible to rule anyway, at least, as far as 'the crown passing to the king's blood-related heir' and all."

"Packs go through power switches every day when an Alpha is defeated in battle. You could always fight for your crown."

She nodded, adding a half-shrug. "Sure, I could. I've thought about it." She took a breath. "But I don't want to be High Queen."

He blinked. "Is this because of me? Because you know how I feel about ruling?"

She chuckled. "Not really. To be honest, I've never wanted the crown." She looked at her feet. "I've actually always wanted to be a veterinarian."

A brow arched and his face slowly lit up in a smile. "I could see that. You're a natural defender. I could see you wanting to look after injured creatures."

"That dream wasn't good enough for my mother," she said quietly, noting it still stung to talk about her. It would take a long time for that to go away, regardless of how she felt about her. "I took some classes when I could, but for the most part, I'd given up on that dream because I never thought it could be a reality. I might have lost my family"—her voice hitched as she said it aloud—"but at the same time, I've been given a chance to pursue my own dreams. For the first time in my life, I can be myself and not feel bad about it."

She cupped his face in her hands, speaking more fervently. "Nik, I'm not going to lie. When I first met you, I thought you were one of the most arrogant men I'd ever met."

He grinned. "Sounds about right."

"But," she said with a smile, "as I got to know you, I was surprised to find a lot of myself in you. You've been hiding who you really are from the world, too. No one saw you, but I did. Just as you were the first to look upon me and not see a princess, but the woman underneath." Her heart skipped a beat as she thought about what she was about to say next. "And, at the risk of sounding like a sap, I've fallen head over heels in love with you."

His breath caught.

"Or at least," she added quickly, "I think I have. Honestly, I had no idea what real love felt like—until now. This, what's happening between us, is something special. And I never, ever want to let that go."

No more than a second passed before his mouth was on hers, kissing her so passionately she could hardly breathe. His tongue raked along hers, caressing it. She moaned, wrapping her arms around his neck and pressing her aching breasts against him. She wanted him to touch her, to suck on her hardened nipples and kiss her in places she'd never been kissed before. She wanted to be ravished, to feel what it was like not having any barriers between them.

"I want to feel you inside me," she said raggedly, starting to take off his robe.

He chuckled and grasped her hands, stopping her. "And believe me, love, no one wants that more than me. But we have to get the paperwork out of the way first, so to speak."

He looked at the door. Alara knew he was silently calling to the people waiting outside. A moment later, Gage and Danica walked in.

Danica smiled at her. "You look beautiful."

"Thank you," Alara said, blushing. She'd almost forgotten about this part. *Right, you mean the part where you have sex for the first time ever in front of a live audience? Totally understandable you'd forget a small detail like that.*

Her stomach felt queasy, and Nik grasped her hand. "You sure about this?" he asked quietly.

Shoving her nerves aside, she nodded. "Yeah," she

said, her voice breathier, "I'm sure."

"Good," Gage said, stepping forward. "Let us begin."

He read them the Rites of the Mates, where they swore their loyalty to one another for all eternity. Strangely enough, when Alara said her vows to Nik, she felt surer. By the time they'd sliced their palms for the blood oath, she'd forgotten all about why she had been nervous in the first place.

Gage gestured for them to proceed to the mating bed, then he and Danica began to softly chant the incantation that would initiate the mating bond. Alara's blood hummed with anticipation as Nik scooped her up into his arms and carried her over to the bed. He laid her down with tender care and began untying the belt that held her robe shut. His eyes never left hers. She saw a mixture of love and lust there, the same look she undoubtedly had.

Shivers raced across her body as he opened the robe and cool air hit her bare skin. Nik stared at her, raw hunger consuming his expression. His eyes roved over her naked body, resting on her breasts. They heaved up and down as her breaths became more ragged as carnal need filled her. Her nipples were erect, waiting to be teased.

In a few fluid motions, he'd removed his robe and cast it aside. The many candles around the room lit up his beautiful, muscular body with a soft yellow glow. Alara forgot all about the scars, not even seeing them as he leaned forward, crawling over her like a predator about to take down his prey.

She felt the hard length of him graze her sex, and her breath lodged in her throat.

"Not yet," he whispered, nuzzling her neck. "I need to prepare you first."

What did he mean? Was this what people called foreplay?

Nerves tingled in her tummy as he began kissing her neck, her nipples raking across his bare chest. He reached up and began kneading her breasts, their fullness barely fitting in the palms of his hands. The first time his tongue flicked out to lick her cherry nubs, she forgot about the people watching and that this was her first time lying with a man. She forgot about anything except how to breathe and the feel of his hands and tongue lighting her skin on fire.

She moaned as his mouth trailed farther down, kissing her from her breasts to below her navel.

When she finally had a moment of clarity among the dizzying sensations swirling within her, she almost told him to stop.

Then he kissed her *there*.

Pleasure shot straight to her core, and she dug her nails into the mattress, clinging to the bed sheets as his lips sucked on her while his tongue explored her sex. Her thighs spread farther as her body relaxed, allowing him to go deeper. She cried out, shoots of pleasure making it feel like every nerve ending in her body was tingling.

At last, when she thought she couldn't take anymore and she'd come undone altogether, Nik sat up and positioned himself over her.

"This will hurt," he said gently, regret shining in his eyes.

"I know," she breathed, barely able to speak. "I'm ready."

He didn't look convinced. Or maybe he was worried about hurting her. She smiled, brushing her fingers along his face as she leaned forward. "Take me, Nik," she whispered. "Join us together, forever."

He let out a shaking breath. Slowly, gently, he lowered himself into her. His shaft was white-hot, stretching her bit by exquisite bit. She sighed as he filled her up.

"Are you all right?" he said quietly.

She nodded. "Farther. I want to feel all of you."

He pressed his hips against hers, making himself glide in farther. There was a great pressure, then a pinch, and suddenly he was wholly in. She gasped, not from pain, but from the incredible bolt of pleasure that rippled through her. His blazing hot sex rubbed her most sensitive spot deep within, and she clawed at his back as he groaned, relishing the feeling. He kissed her as he gently began rocking himself in and out, sweet gestures that were no less scorching than their earlier kisses.

She rocked with him, bringing her hips up to meet his time and time again, building momentum as the fire in her increased. Blue light shone through the room, radiating from the tattoos forming along their torsos, chests, backs, and arms, but her pleasure-addled mind barely registered what was happening.

Her world was unraveling—*she* was unraveling.

She could tell he was too. His breaths became ragged, and he clung to her hips, gripping them as he made love to her more urgently.

"Nik," she gasped, right before the light reached its climax. Fireworks sparked in her vision as she squeezed her eyes shut and cried out as pleasure surged through her, emanating from a spot deep within.

A moment later, Nik grunted, coming hard as he pumped a few more times before stilling. He lay on top of her, both of them soaked in sweat and breathing hard.

In a state of blissful delirium, she blinked the stars out of her vision and observed her arms. Intricate tattoos of midnight blue inked her skin from one arm to the next, as it did on her mate's.

Her mate's.

She couldn't help the smile that broke out across her face. "It worked."

Nik kissed her, looking amused. "You seem surprised."

"It's just… I was so afraid…."

"Sssh." He kissed her forehead and brushed the sweat-dampened hair from her face. "There's nothing to be afraid of. I won't ever leave you. I swear to be loyal to you, always." He rested his forehead against hers. "We're a family now."

A family.

Tears stung her eyes. "Oh, Nik."

Someone tried hiding a cough without much success. Alara looked past Nik's shoulder, where Danica was blushing sheepishly. "Crap," she said under her breath. "I was trying not to ruin the mood."

Nik grinned, sitting up and retrieving his robe. He helped Alara get dressed, but not before taking one last eyeful of her in. "I'll never get tired of that," he murmured.

"Careful," Alara whispered, trailing a nail down his chest. "Or you'll get horny again."

"Already there, sweetheart." He cleared his throat and turned to smile at Danica. "No harm done, love. The ceremony was perfect." He sat behind Alara, pulling her into his lap. "It's probably just as well you interrupted us." He kissed the back of his mate's neck. "She has a meeting to attend tonight anyway."

"About the Crescent Pack leadership, right?" Gage murmured darkly.

Alara nodded. She had told Nik it was all right to divulge the details about her heritage to Gage and Danica. Though Alara had made no official statement yet, she knew it was only a matter of time before the secret came out. She'd rather it be from her own mouth than through some scandal the tabloids made up.

"I'm going to announce my true lineage and relinquish my hold on the crown," Alara said strongly. "Once that happens, the werewolf community can move forward with electing a new High King."

Gage ran a hand over his face. "This is going to be a bloodbath. Every Alpha in the country will be going after this position once they hear the news."

"Not if I name a successor," Alara said. "I'm still half-royal. There's a clause that states I can name a successor. He or she can be challenged for the crown, sure, but my naming my own candidate will give him or her enormous political sway."

"You sure about that, love?" Nik said gently. "You know how the royals love to shun halflings."

153

He didn't mean it as an insult. It was the bitter truth. Oh, yes, she knew all too well how those stuck-up lot treated people they deemed below them. "Most of them respect me enough I think to at least listen to what I have to say. My father wasn't the only one who knew how to build connections."

Nik grinned. "That's my girl."

"Okay, so say they will back you," Gage said. "That's an enormous responsibility, not to mention a lot of power. Who exactly are you going to get to accept such a candidacy?"

"Actually," Alara began carefully, "I already have someone in mind." She looked Gage right in the eyes.

"I want to name you my successor."

END OF BOOK 2

Read the continuation of Danica and Gage's story in *Betrayal*, now available!

OTHER BOOKS BY
LOLA TAYLOR

The Her Dark Desires Trilogy
Carnal (free for a limited time!)
Sinful
Soulful (coming soon!)

Blood Moon Rising
Fever (free for a limited time!)
Protector
Betrayal
Captured
Sacrifice
Ritual

Blood Moon Rising companion novels
Lust
Forever (coming soon!)

Standalone novels
Shatter

For a full list of titles, please visit
www.lolataylorbooks.com.

For more information, please visit
www.lolataylorbooks.com

Your opinion matters—please leave a review!

Thank you for reading my book! If you have a moment, I'd really appreciate an honest rating and review. They help authors stand out in a busy marketplace, plus they give browsing readers the nitty gritty on books they're shopping. Everyone wins when you rate and review, so please do! Your opinion counts!

ABOUT THE AUTHOR

"Lola Taylor" is a pen name created for the romances I can't show my grandma without blushing. My favorite genre to write is romantic suspense, usually involving hot werewolves, warlocks, or any other type of paranormal creature. Keep the action hot and the romance hotter—that's my motto! I'm a horror film junkie, I still love Halloween as an adult (seriously, I think I get more excited for it than some kids do), and what precious spare time I have is spent with my family, reading (everything from sci fi to middle grade), playing the flute, painting pretty pictures, or screwing around on Pinterest or Etsy. Hailing from the South, I currently live in the Midwest with five fur babies and my hubby.

You can connect with me on Facebook (www.facebook. com/lolataylorbooks) or my email (lolawritespnr@gmail. com). Learn more about me and my books at www. lolataylorbooks.com.